THE DRAGON HUNT

THE DRAGON

HUNT FIVE STORIES

TRAN VU

TRANSLATED FROM THE
VIETNAMESE BY
NINA MCPHERSON
AND
PHAN HUY DUONG

HYPERION EAST

NEW YORK

The translators would like to thank the many people in Vietnam and in Paris who read, corrected, and commented on these stories. We are particularly grateful to Tran Dinh, Hoang Ngoc Hien, Tri Nguyen, and Nguyen Thi Binh, without whom much more would have been lost in translation.

We also thank the author for reviewing and helping craft these translations, most notably the adaptation of "The Coral Reef," first published in *Granta: Fifty* (Summer 1995).

A slightly different version of the translation of the story "Gunboat on the Yangtze" appeared in the anthology *Night, Again: Contemporary Fiction from Vietnam*, edited by Linh Dinh (New York: Seven Stories Press, 1996).

Library of Congress Cataloging-in-Publication Data

Trân Vũ

The dragon hunt / Trân Vũ ; translated from the Vietnamese by Nina McPherson.

p.   cm.

Contents: The coral reef—Gunboat on the Yangtze—The back street of Hoi An—Nha Nam—The dragon hunt.

ISBN 0-7868-6418-4

I. Title.

PL4378.9.T6922D7   1999

895.9'22334—dc21   98-19994
                                    CIP

Design by Jill Gogal
First Edition
10 9 8 7 6 5 4 3 2 1

CONTENTS

THE DRAGON HUNT

THE CORAL REEF

MAY 28, 1979

"So, this is our last night of socialism," Dzung said as he squatted down beside me. I pulled two cigarettes out of my pocket and handed one to him, but didn't reply. Instead, I nudged my little brother, Bien, and sent him off to find somewhere to sleep in the house behind us. We had been told to assemble there and wait for the boat, the boat that was going to take us away from Vietnam.

After Bien had left, I spoke. "When my mother gave the boat owner her gold, he said there were going to be two hundred of us. A few days ago, there were two hundred and fifty. Now look—there are at least three hundred people on the quay, and the police are sure to try to squeeze more on at the last minute. It's going to be packed."

Dzung sighed and lit his cigarette.

The voyage from My Tho had been postponed many times, either by the police or by Truong Hong, the boat owner. Each time we had returned, miserable, to Saigon. But tonight was different. Tomorrow, the MT603, claimed by Truong Hong to be the safest vessel in the region, was due to sail. No one wanted to miss it.

"Dzung, why are you leaving?" I asked abruptly, flicking my cigarette ash into the gutter.

"Same reason as you," he said. "I've got to get out of here, even if I have to crawl on my hands and knees."

"Why?"

Dzung seemed surprised. "That's simple. I can't stand the meetings every night of the week. I don't want to do any more irrigation work. I can't bear to see my friends being sent off to some godforsaken hole in Cambodia to die. I refuse to be condemned to a life of reading party newspapers."

The reasons were so obvious that no one bothered to go into them anymore. People just left. Dzung and I had been born into communism. We had had it with Marx, Lenin, and the Soviet economy, and with theorizing about why we wanted to leave. We only knew that we had to go.

Most of the people waiting for the boat were Chinese, or of Chinese origin, like us. Because of the border war with China, the Vietnamese government was only too happy to see us go.

That night Dzung and I didn't sleep, and neither did anyone else. People sat on little stools, chattering in singsong Cantonese. They hadn't read *Das Kapital* or the complete works of Lenin, but they knew, from their own wretched lives and the terror of last year's purges, that they too had to go.

MAY 29

Late in the afternoon, a Peugeot pulled up in front of the house, and a policeman got out. He was wearing gold-rimmed glasses and a Rolex. He had come to talk to Truong Hong.

The atmosphere in the house grew more tense. *Let's go, let's go.* Eventually, Truong Hong divided us into fifteen groups, and we set off toward the quay.

Suddenly, a shout arose from the crowd.

"Look!"

"The boat—it's there!"

Unable to contain ourselves, we broke ranks and ran toward the river. There were three large wooden boats moored along the quay.

"Which is the MT603?"

"The red one."

"My God, how are we going to stay afloat in that tiny thing?"

Truong Hong had disappeared. Rumors spread through the crowd: the boat was heading for Australia; it was going only as far as the South Pacific; the BBC was reporting pirate attacks in the Gulf of Siam; the Voice of America was saying Malaysia, Indonesia, and Singapore were refusing to accept refugees and were towing their boats back into the open sea. I didn't understand. How could our Asian neighbors send us back to our deaths?

About an hour later, Truong Hong reappeared with the policeman, who was carrying a megaphone.

"Attention! Attention! On behalf of the Party Secretary, on behalf of the police, I would like to say a few words before you leave." He made a speech full of exhortations to work hard in foreign lands and guard our ancient heroic tradition. Then finally:

"These are the individuals authorized to board the MT603. Group One: leader, Mr. Lam Hue; members, Trong Sieu, Dang Cam, Phung Tao—"

"That's you! Go!" Dzung elbowed me. "Phung Tao—that's the name on your birth certificate."

"Here!" I yelled, jumping to my feet.

One by one we boarded the boat, sailors herding us down ramps into the hold, which was airless and gloomy, lit only by a single storm lantern.

"Move along, ten to a bench!" the sailors yelled.

"They're packing us in like sardines," said Dzung. "I just heard someone say that the police have sent another hundred people."

Bien and I, both under eighteen, were assigned places on the middle deck, with the women. At least there were portholes here, I thought: an escape route if the boat began to sink. I slipped my hand through the nearest one, then snatched it back in shock: the water was only twenty centimeters below.

It was almost midnight, and the boat was still moored by the quay. No one knew what was happening. Truong Hong and the skipper had gone back into town, presumably to split their gold with the police. I slept fitfully. Whenever I woke, I peered out of the porthole. The boat hadn't moved.

May 30

I was asleep when we set sail. Two police patrol boats escorted the MT603 out to sea, and I was woken by the police shouting through a megaphone, wishing us bon voyage before circling back to the harbor.

As dawn broke, I watched the muddy red water race past on the other side of the porthole. Here, where the river met the sea, conflicting currents joined, making powerful waves that slapped against the hull, sending the boat into a drunken reel. We plowed east, heading for the Philippines, for Australia.

After a few hours, people began to be seasick. The

woman next to me was soon slimy with vomit. Old women squatted on the floor to urinate. The stench was suffocating, but the high, crashing waves made opening the portholes impossible.

I went down to the lower deck, where the situation was even worse. Stuck inside the prow, it was as though the waves were pounding at my chest, pummeling me. The hold bore the brunt of the turbulence. The storm lantern had gone out, leaving the people there in darkness, awash in stomach-turning smells.

June 2

By the fourth day people were beginning to feel better, though the sea was no calmer. They got out bags of rich food and ate noisily. They vomited, they ate, they pissed, they shat. The stench was so bad that I decided to try to go out on deck. I had to step over people to reach the door, accidentally kicking an old woman in the head as I went.

"Get down!" yelled a sailor on the ramp, forcing me back below.

"Just let me go and piss," I begged, struggling to get free.

"Piss down there, like everyone else!" shouted the sailor.

"It's OK. Let him through." Truong Do, the boat owner's son, was pulling me up. "Go on, but come straight back. Understand?"

I said nothing and climbed up to the main deck. The toilets were at the back of the boat. There was no one there. My bladder was bursting. There was a hole in the floor, through which I could see the churning water below. What if a huge wave knocked me into it? The fear paralyzed me. I couldn't piss. I went back outside. The wind howled around me.

"Get back here!" the sailor shouted. He tried to kick me; I seized his foot, and he went sprawling on the deck. I ran off, back toward the lavatories, the sailor lumbering after me. Suddenly, the boat keeled sharply to one side, throwing both of us off balance. There was a sound of cracking, splintering wood, and screams of terror rose from below. The sailor and I forgot our struggle; we were hypnotized by the pitching of the vessel. I could see the skipper fighting to regain control of the boat as it rolled and shuddered. Over the crashing of the waves and the roar of the engines rose the prayers of four hundred people.

"The propeller is caught in the net!" someone cried.

The skipper tried to accelerate, but the boat reeled again, tipped violently to one side, as though it was about to capsize. People began shouting.

"Rocks!"

"Reverse, reverse!"

"Turn on the back-up engines. Accelerate!"

"Throw the baggage overboard! We're overloaded!"

The boat wouldn't move forward, even with the engines at full throttle, their noise almost drowned out by the shrieking and wailing of the passengers. The sailors began to throw bags into the seething ocean.

In the cabin, the skipper and Truong Hong were arguing furiously, one convinced the boat had run aground, the other adamant that it was snared in nets. It seemed incredible that there could be rocks here, in the middle of the sea, but clearly we had run up against something. The engines howled. The deck bucked again and again, until it seemed the boat might split in two.

The MT603 had now tipped completely to one side, its edge submerged in water. Everyone was ordered to stand to the right to restore the balance. Panic-stricken, the sailors were dumping things overboard indiscriminately: sacks of provisions, jerry cans of drinking water.

The skipper and the chief engineer tried again, hoping that now the load was lighter, we would float, but the engine had barely whined before the prow reared up and fell back onto rocks with a terrible crunch. We listened, petrified by the cracking of the beams supporting the deck as, one by one, they gave way, crushing the cabins crammed full of people below.

Arms flailed like tentacles through the portholes, trying to get a grip on the hull. People were jumping overboard. Some were struggling through the wreckage to get to the sealed cabins, where we could hear the screams of the trapped women and children. Driven by some instinct, I jumped into the sea. Before I left home, my mother had given me a U.S. Army-surplus life jacket and made me promise to wear it throughout the voyage; I was glad now that I had kept my word. I felt the soles of my feet being shredded as I hit coral.

The sun rose, dazzling, magnificent, in the Pacific sky.

June 3

The MT603 had run aground on a coral reef. The desolate wreck lay surrounded by the glistening ocean, in limbo between sky and earth. I swam around the boat and eventually found Dzung and Bien, who had managed to smash their way out of the hold.

Under the burning sun the sea took on different colors. At the back of the boat the water was a deep emerald, but toward the prow it turned pale. The coral reef seemed immense, and, judging from the shade of the water, the boat had run aground about twenty meters inside it.

"We've had it," Dzung said, paddling about. "The boat's stuck. What can we do?"

There were about four hundred people in the water, each proposing a different solution for saving the boat. Miraculously, no one had been killed, and only nine had been injured.

The water was bracing, invigorating after days of sweat and filth. Although it was shallow, the sea was rough, and waves kept knocking us over. Razor-sharp coral clawed our legs.

Truong Hong, brandishing a megaphone he had somehow salvaged, took charge. He ordered everyone into the fifteen groups we had been assigned to when we first boarded the boat. We were going to attempt to maneuver it back into the sea. The strongest men were to push the prow, while the rest of us took the sides. Women and children were told to keep out of the way, while the injured, the skipper, and the engineer stayed on board.

"At the count of three, push hard. One, two, three, push!"

"Again—push!"

"One, two, three, push! Push!"

"Why aren't those bastards back there pushing?"

The men and the boys braced themselves, muscles flexed, feet firmly planted on the jagged coral, pushing with all their might. But we had no lever, no fulcrum, no means of getting a purchase. We were exhausting ourselves for nothing. The MT603 stayed put, wedged at a sixty-degree angle, waves smacking against it.

As the sun set, the tide went out, revealing an island of coral as far as the eye could see. The water receded quickly; soon it was only ankle deep. Only then did I realize the terrible truth: even when the tide was in, the water would be too shallow for the boat to float. The wreck of the MT603 would never get off the reef.

Night fell. We were cold and exhausted. Everyone's

skin, pickled in salt water, was shriveled. We clambered back onto the boat, where I collapsed, shivering.

We huddled together for warmth. I rolled up my trousers, exposing my torn legs and feet to the air; they had stopped bleeding, but the flesh was swollen and bruised violet. I no longer felt any pain, only an insistent, biting prickle.

"Bastards! They've taken all the food," said Bien, emerging from the hold, his thin body silhouetted against the crimson sky. "Truong Hong and the rest of them have got all the provisions. This is all I could find."

My brother's voice was weary, bitter. He threw down two packets of rice, a pack of dried bananas, a sachet of tea. It seemed to me that his face, with its blackened skin, had aged since yesterday; he was almost unrecognizable.

"Oh, who cares," said Dzung. "In two weeks we'll all be dead anyway."

We sat cross-legged in a circle to share our meager meal, chewing each mouthful slowly, painfully. Already, less than twenty-four hours after the shipwreck, we were utterly changed.

Emergency flares flickered in the dark, spreading an eerie light over the wreckage. By the time the moon cast its cold glow across the ocean, most of us were asleep. The wind blew all night, drowning out the sobs and moans of the children, soothing the pain of our lacerated flesh.

• • • •

The next day, the fifteen groups disbanded. We Vietnamese-Chinese elected a man named Ly, a former lieutenant captain in the army, to be our leader. Most of the others remained faithful to Truong Hong; those who did not kept to themselves, refusing to help in our efforts to shift the boat. They spent their time searching for coral for the food that had been thrown overboard, and took turns guarding the bags they had managed to rescue.

Two teams of volunteers, armed with hammers, attempted to free the propellers by diving down and smashing the coral that trapped them. Ly had suggested cutting down one of the masts to use as a lever, which we propped under the boat.

"One, two, three, push!"

The wreck rose slowly, as if it were finding its balance.

"It's coming up, it's coming up—"

But suddenly the MT603 keeled back on its side, sending the men holding the lever flying onto the coral. The boat came to rest in its old position. We were up to our necks in water, and the coral had reopened the cuts on our feet.

For a moment it seemed the boat had shifted a little, half a meter, perhaps even a whole one, but that night, as the tide receded, making the reef appear to rise like a sea monster from the waves, we realized that it was the water level that had moved, not the boat. The MT603 hadn't budged an inch.

"There'll be a big tide in a few days," said Ly. "Let's wait."

He believed the reef to be one of the notorious Paracel Islands, which stretch for several hundred miles. Not boat dares venture near them. He calculated that we were four or five days away from the Philippines.

When we clambered onto the boat that night, the clouds seemed darker, more threatening. Fear tightened around us like a noose.

JUNE 7

Two days later, we found a corpse. It was a woman whose back had been broken when the main deck collapsed. I watched as some men bound the body to a piece of wood which they pushed out to sea.

In the days that followed, there were more deaths— from exhaustion, from despair. Two corpses in particular haunted me: one of an old man whose stomach had swollen grotesquely, and one of a strangely wizened child who had died during a seizure. The boat owner and his family lit incense and prayed over them, the scent from the joss sticks wafting across the deck.

We marked the number of people left on the reef with SOS buoys which we threw into the sea each time someone died: 394, 391, 388. . . . Each day fewer and fewer men had the strength to push the boat. Today, nine days after we set sail, our seventh day on the reef, no one came at all.

The food and water had more or less run out. A couple of us tried to boil sea water and distill the vapor. We spent three hours hunched over a liter of oily, salty fluid, confident of our school science, but it was useless; we produced only a few drops of water we could drink. We stared at the clouds, desperate for rain. Occasionally, there were unexpected storms that blew up in minutes. We scavenged for rice in the wreck. We had to survive, so we survived.

JUNE 8

Five of us—Dzung, Bien, the boat owner's two sons, and I—decided that we had to take our chances and get off the reef. We built two makeshift rafts—just planks bound together with rope, perched on empty water containers and kept afloat by buoys. When we sat on them, the water came up to waist level.

We tried to paddle at first, but after a while we tied our tiny rafts loosely together and let them drift, following the currents, tossing with the waves which were about to tip us into the water at any moment. We hadn't really considered the insanity of setting off on a few pieces of wood lashed together. Our only aim had been to escape the slow death that awaited us on the reef.

When it began to get dark, we grew frightened. It was very cold. Blanketed in fog, we listened to the rhythms of the current as it sucked us farther into the night. The wind howled. But we were off the reef—

earlier in the day, when the sun still warmed the sea, I had dived down and had seen no coral.

The sea was now calmer from time to time. We checked the knots on the ropes binding the rafts together, but otherwise we just drifted. I glanced at the Truong brothers; they were wide-eyed, pale, and vacant. They evidently regretted having come with us.

I was transfixed by the immensity of the sky and the sea, unaware of anything else, when suddenly I felt an invisible force tugging the rafts and saw a black shape sliding underneath them. At first I thought we were running onto rocks and cried out to warn the others. But then I realized that the black shape was moving at the same speed as us.

"What is it?" whispered Dzung.

Mesmerized, we all stared, unable to take our eyes off it.

"Probably just rocks. It's nothing. Let's get out of here," mumbled Truong Doc, clinging to the buoys, drawing his knees up to his neck.

"The sea is really deep here; it can't be a rock," I said.

The black shape continued to slide alongside and underneath us, the white foam swirling in its wake. Then, through the fog, a triangle appeared—a huge, pointed fin, gliding toward us.

"My God, Bien, it's a shark!" I cried as the fin whipped the water less than three meters away. The waves it raised sent the rafts spinning. Panicked, I seized the paddle to defend myself. Dzung, Bien, and the Truong brothers trembled convulsively, their prayers choking in their throats.

"Don't touch it!" I screamed, trying to get a grip on myself. My brother shrieked. The fin turned, moving closer, circling the rafts. It was no longer alone; there were five or six others. They plunged and resurfaced, slicing the sea and the night, scattering thousands of tiny, sparkling waves in their wake. They played at this for a half hour or so and then disappeared. It took us a long time to regain our calm.

"Probably whales," Dzung panted.

As the danger receded, we stared ahead into the darkness, imagining fins lying in wait behind every wave. We drifted on and on, losing all sense of time. Our minds were entirely taken up by our contest with the sea. Suddenly, out of nowhere, an enormous wave raised us to its crest and hurled us back down.

"We're sinking!"

Our cries floated over the deserted sea. No echoes. Only the waves thundered in response; they seemed even more threatening in the dark.

"The waves!" Dzung shouted. "I can hear the waves hitting a shore."

"We must be near the coast," I said, stunned.

"Impossible," Bien said. "We haven't been gone a day."

"Maybe it's a deserted island," I said.

We watched as the silvery foam rose and fell. We

were being dragged into a current. Rocks rose out of nowhere, and a strong swell threw the raft against them, almost crushing the Truong brothers.

"Push!"

"Watch out, there are more rocks on the left!"

A massive wave reared up in front of us, curling slowly inward before crashing down on the rafts. Sucked up out of the water, we were flung backward, clinging to the fraying rope that bound our rafts together. Then I felt my feet touch coral: we were back where we had started, run aground on the reef.

We paddled furiously, clinging to what was left of the rafts, dodging outcrops of coral, straining to gulp in air between avalanches of water. I remembered what Ly had said about the coral archipelago extending for hundreds of miles.

We fought the waves and rocks for what seemed like hours, but as the dawn came, a current swept us off the reef, and we were once again carried toward deep water. Finally, we slept, lulled by the rhythm of the waves, drifting, unconscious, kept afloat by our life jackets and the buoys we'd tied to ourselves.

I awoke to feel my face swollen by sunburn. The sun, enormous, incandescent, scorched our skin. I roused the others, and we searched for the ten-liter water can that Truong Hong had kept hidden in the hold and then given to his sons, but it had been carried off by the waves. No more water meant certain death. Unable to bear the heat, we plunged into the sea. Bien's lips were bloated and blistered, the skin peeling off them. I began to feel weak, delirious even, as I imagined myself on dry land by a water pump. The sun pounded down. More coral, more waves, nothing but these rafts and our wrinkled bodies drifting east.

Later that day, a storm broke. In a few seconds black clouds covered the sky. The wind howled over our heads, and rain fell, stinging our faces and whipping at the surging sea. Clinging to the buoys, we were plunged into what seemed like a huge whirlpool. I have no idea how long the tempest lasted, but as the sea eventually grew calmer we could dimly make out, through a dense curtain of rain, the silhouette of a boat. The storm had carried us back to the shipwreck.

JUNE 10

The MT603 was in an even worse state than it had been when we left. The main deck had collapsed farther, and five people had been killed. All that remained of the safest boat in the region was the skipper's cabin, the prow, and the stern.

Ly wanted to know exactly what had happened to us. Everyone else was angry and just asked about the disappearance of the ten-liter water can.

"You invented that trip just to get the water! You didn't even try to get help!"

The next morning, we tried once more to push the wreckage, without success. We threw the last emergency buoy overboard, inscribed with the number of survivors: 382. Everyone watched it until it disappeared. I had lost all hope: the buoys were probably stuck somewhere in the middle of the immense coral archipelago.

Since the shipwreck we hadn't seen a single airplane or ship. Without the Pacific rains we would never have survived. Every day, as the tide went out, I joined the scrawny phantoms who scoured the reef in search of food, but the coral sea was a dead sea: no shrimp, no shellfish, nothing. Once we found a starfish and a few strands of seaweed, which we boiled up with a bit of rainwater, but the seaweed was gluey and disgusting, the starfish rigid, impossible to eat.

JUNE 12

Ly had decided to try his luck on a raft. He bound four planks together, attached them to empty barrels, and covered them with a tarpaulin on which he had painted the letters SOS. He set off at noon with his wife and two young children, heading for Hong Kong.

That night, a further eighteen people, mostly sailors, left in two groups on similar rafts, taking the last of the buoys.

JUNE 14

The big tide that Ly had predicted on the first day finally arrived. It was night, and the moon was full.

Since sundown we had been standing in the icy water, watching the horizon, waiting for a miracle. In the chill moonlight I could no longer distinguish women from men, or adults from children: everyone looked old, shriveled, covered from head to toe with blisters and sores. I remembered how I had promised my mother to take care of my brother, to make a man out of him. I felt plagued with guilt and regret when I thought of the gold she had handed over to buy us places on the boat.

Suddenly, a huge wave slapped me against the coral. It was the tide, the big tide.

"Push! Push!"

The sea reared up, the water rising from our waists to our chests. Seven men pushed with all their strength. The water rose to our chins. Almost totally submerged, we fought to free the boat. People with children clambered, terrified, onto what remained of the main deck. Dzung and I hung onto the sides. As the water came over our heads, I pulled myself up, landing in a heap on the deck, which was slick with oil. The boat hadn't moved.

Suddenly, we were flung to the right. I felt the boat rear and then pitch wildly to the left and back again. Then it seemed to regain its equilibrium, achieving a position we had no longer believed possible, floating in deep water.

"Skipper, turn on the engines!"

"Reverse, reverse quickly!"

The engines sputtered, the men yelled, the women

prayed, but the boat didn't move. The coral reef was no longer visible, swallowed under the black depths of the water, but still it held the boat in its grasp.

"You young people will have to get off," the skipper ordered. "We've got to lighten the load."

Women took up the cry. I felt myself lifted into the air and passed from hand to hand to the edge of the boat. I struggled, resisted, but they pushed me overboard.

"We'll come back and get you when the boat is free!" the skipper shouted.

I had barely caught my breath when I felt a violent current dragging me around the wreck. The surface of the water was bleached with foam: we were being sucked toward the spinning propellers. I flailed, trying to cling to the slippery hull. I grabbed hold of someone's foot and then a rope that hung down from the skipper's cabin. Eventually, we were pulled back on board.

I collapsed on deck, vomiting sea water. When I opened my eyes, the sky had cleared: the clouds seemed brighter, the wind more gentle. Twenty of us had been thrown into the sea; four had disappeared; one had drowned. The coral archipelago had disappeared back into the ocean. A woman began to sob.

The MT603 moved toward the sun.

Gunboat on the
Yangtze

One day Toan comes up behind me, covers my head with a black veil, and says: "Sometimes you can see through a blindfold."

And with these enigmatic words he leaves. I turn around. The veil wriggles, snaking around his hand. Like a dance.

"It's the invisible that really excites."

Words. Always incomprehensible, ambiguous. The veil writhes, opens into a fan, pulses like a bat's wing, slithers and bends like a dead snake. A kind of cobra.

An idea flashes through my mind: Toan is a cobra poised, ready to attack me. Already he approaches, flicking the veil skillfully, like a matador. He folds it into a blindfold and pulls it over my eyes.

"Can you see anything, Elder sister?"

His face is so close I can feel every breath, hot, against my cheeks.

"Nothing."

Violently he pulls the blindfold tighter.

"Can you see now?"

I shake my head. He pulls it tighter. My eyes burn.

"It's only when we're in pain that we take the trouble to think."

He yanks the ends of the blindfold. I can't see him, but I feel the sweat from his clammy wrists against my face, imagine his arm muscles flexing. The blindfold tightens, crushing my temples.

"That's enough!"

My scream, in an instant, dissipates the humid, suffocating atmosphere of the room. Groping, I undo the blindfold. The black veil falls, unfurls on the floor, dead, like a snake's corpse. My eyes still smart. Toan has slunk into a corner. He plays his favorite tune on the cello. The music resonates, note by note, phrase by phrase, scale by scale, by turns grave, strident, haunting.

Toan is seated, his head slumped on his chest. He steals a sidelong glance at me with his misshapen eyes. He saws feverishly on the cello with the bow, his left arm wrapped around its round, voluptuous body, clutching it passionately, as a man would embrace a woman. The bow advances, retreats, relentless. The cello squeaks like an old saw scraping steel wire. A dull, plodding, tortured sound permeates the room, swallows the bookcase, the dining table, crawls right up to me.

"That's enough!"

I shout again. I can't stand this malicious, sinister look, his amorphous gaze. Suddenly the cello falls silent. The bow slides off the strings.

"Are you forbidding me to play, or to look at you?" Toan snaps.

"Both."

"That's right. We're just stones, blocks of wood."

He snickers and disappears into his room.

I stay there, alone, anxious.

For a long time now, Toan has lived abnormally in a strange, dark world, a world that encloses him. But tonight this odd game has turned serious. What's worse, I know why, guess the root of the strangeness. I wipe his clammy sweat from my cheek that, for all this time, has been seeping into my skin. When I got into my room, I can hear the sound of Toan thrashing about in his. I pull the covers over my head, trying to block out the writhing of a body tortured by loneliness. But from under the blankets, in the darkness that engulfs me, I see it again: that night Toan wanted to make me see.

$\bullet \quad \bullet \quad \bullet$

Daylight came, I woke up late, haggard, I hadn't slept
at all, had just lain there on my back, holding my head
in my hands staring into the black veil. It was a bleak
Sunday morning. Toan's silhouette is engraved in my
door frame. Outside, skeleton-like trees strained their
thin arms toward the sky, as if to ask for divine grace.
I move toward the kitchen table for my breakfast: coffee, one sugar cube. Toan always takes care of breakfast. Every morning he places one sugar cube next to
my coffee cup, and I understand.

"When you came here, you told me you wouldn't
leave me, that you would live for me and for me alone.
Do you remember?" he says, detecting my presence.

"I remember."

"So, what are you waiting for? Who sacrificed himself for you?"

"You did." I respond mechanically, unable to look
up into his face. Slowly he approaches, behind my
back, as he did the night before, and plasters his hands
over my eyes.

"Stop!"

I struggle to free myself, from his fingers, from the
night. Toan's breath on my hair is heavy, staggered,
panting.

"Stop, please stop."

His fingers slowly relax, press my temples, fondle
my cheek, brush against my chin, massage my neck. I
shudder; his two hands grip me hard like pincers. He

keeps pummeling me, sometimes violent, sometimes caressing. I shudder and shove him away.

"That's enough. Stop!"

"*That's enough.* That's all you can say."

He turns me around, runs his finger down the bridge of my nose to my lips, stops there. I watch myself yield, accept his games. Why? So he won't despair, won't destroy himself.

"Do you know how to kiss?" Toan asks.

Suddenly his face falls. The scar across his lip deepens. Panicked, I fling myself on his chest, spill his cup of coffee on me, over the couch. He grabs my face, pulling it toward his lips.

"You've seen movies, so you must know how to kiss."

"That's enough!"

His shredded, scarred lips grope for me, I turn my face away, they fall onto my cheek, prickly, at once dry and clammy. His mouth sticks to my cheek, he burrows his head in the curve of my neck, refuses to let go. I don't resist anymore. My body is soaked with coffee. I hug him to me. I feel no horror as I touch his shattered face, the puffy ridges of skin between the gashes. I pity him.

"That's enough now. Go play your cello."

He looks at me, indifferent, distant, as he does every time I refuse. But he seems to have softened. Now the cello again, like yesterday evening, grave, distraught, anarchic. Who knows what he hears in this music that he plays day in and day out, month after month. I don't . . . but I know the image he wants me to see through the black veil.

You need a girlfriend, I tell him, when he least expects it, as he is bent over his cello. The cello abruptly falls silent. His misshapen eyes search in my direction.

"What did you say?"

"You need a girlfriend."

"Who would dare love me?"

"I'll find her for you."

Toan stays silent for a long time; then he gets up, moves toward the window, opens it. Wind rushes into the room. The curtains rise and fall, flapping, like butterfly wings impaled on a pin. Toan turns toward me, deliberately exposing his ravaged face to the sun. The scars I once watched go purple under the botched sutures, that I have seen crust and dry under the burning sun of the islands. In the light of day, his shattered face is bizarre, horrible.

"Take a good look, Elder sister. Who could love this face? Do you think I don't know what my face is like? All I have to do is touch it to know that."

He puts his hand to his face; his fingers suddenly arch, his nails claw into the flesh, as if to rip away its hideous shape.

"Toan! Stop it!" I scream, throwing myself onto him, grabbing the fingers that scrape and dig into his face. His body tenses, his back arching as if he wants to flee. He lets out a long, anguished howl. I press my face to his, hug his head to my shoulder, massage his rough, lumpy skin, kiss his scars, comfort him.

"Listen, Toan, don't do that anymore. Ever. Do you hear me? Never again."

"You don't love me."

"I can't. I don't have the right to. . . ."

He hugs me, wraps his arm around my waist. I wait until he calms down, and then gently pry open his arms.

"I'll find you a friend, I swear it." I say, exhausted.

He releases me, sits down at the kitchen table, picks up a book, as if he wants to overcome his emotion. His fingers grope over the Braille, letter by letter, word by word, searching for meaning on this piece of paper. It kills me to watch. Nothing is more painful than watching someone you love die slowly, from the inside. The faces of my girlfriends file past my eyes, then fade into questions, hesitation, doubt, fear. Joelle, Kate, Florence, Isabelle? Any woman will do. As long as it's not me. It can never be me.

Kate comes in, takes off her coat and hat. Her auburn hair tumbles down the line of buttons on the front of her wool dress. She tells me not to go to any trouble, then settles on the couch. She glances around. I know who she's looking for. "Something to drink?" I ask, knowing she rarely does. As expected, she shakes her head. I insist, and she accepts. "It's good when it's cold out," I say, pouring her a glass. I stare at the translucent liquid as she lifts it to her lips, as if I wished it were a kind of potion to steel her courage.

Kate sets the glass on the table, rubs her hands, relaxed now. She's still young, probably the same age as Toan, but she seems very mature. I'm relieved to see her so calm, so relaxed. I've told her about Toan, that he had an accident, how he is forced to live like a recluse, how miserable he is. If she could come see him now and then, maybe on the weekends . . .

Kate politely chats with me about his life, if he likes music, books. We have such a huge bookcase, she remarks. I tell her that Toan is crazy about playing the cello, that the books are mine, that Toan can read only a few books, the kind written for people like him. She is surprised, asks why. I try to explain that Toan doesn't see clearly, that his eyes were wounded. I want to prepare her, but she seems so sure of herself, tells me not to worry.

"I understand. I've been in situations like this. Don't worry. I'm sure we'll be good friends." She takes my arm encouragingly. She seems relaxed, composed. Just then the sound of Toan's cello howls through the room. Kate flinches, her face changes. I'm not surprised. Toan's anarchic, jagged tune, like his sickness, is so familiar to me, and yet each time I hear it, even I find it eerie, chilling.

Still, Kate gets up and asks to meet him. I walk her to Toan's room, knock on the door, announce a friend. He doesn't answer. The cello grates out the same tune.

I push the door open. Toan is seated, his back turned to us. His shoulders heave in time with the cello, with the to and fro of the bow. I hear Kate say, "Hello, Toan," watch her as she enters the room. Toan keeps playing, his head averted, bent over the cello, as if he had heard nothing. I watch Kate as she stands behind him, listening to the music swirl around the room. Suddenly I regret having brought Kate here. I feel confused. Anger and jealousy rise in me. The idea of losing Toan makes me sad, though I know this makes no sense. Kate places her hand on Toan's shoulder.

No one expected what happened. Not me, not Kate, not even him. When Toan slowly turned his head, exposing his ravaged, shriveled flesh, the two holes that masquerade as his eyes, his deformed half nose, the long gash that cuts across his forehead, through his lips, all the way down to his chin, Kate's face froze, her calm turning to panic. She screamed in terror. Her cry paralyzed me. She ran out of the room, fled the house, calling for help. Even after she had run out of the house, her ghoulish scream haunted that corridor for a long time. Toan's cello lay upside down on the floor. Tears streamed from the sockets of his eyes; the gnarled flesh that was once his face was contorted in pain and shame. He wept in silence. But I broke down in sobs, hugged his head to my chest. My tears mingled with his, trickling into those sockets.

"No one can love me. No one will ever be my girl-friend." He moans, and I put my hand over his mouth, tell him I love him, that I will be his girlfriend. I say I'll do anything, anything to save him from this loneliness, so he can live a normal life, like every other normal young man. He asks me why I feel regret, why I resist him. And I tell him that I won't anymore, that I was raped at sea, that I've nothing left to protect anymore.

We coil around each other on the carpet. He nuzzles my hair with his head, weeping silently. I pat his back the way I used to, to console him. That was such a long time ago. Old memories, tender images of our childhood, rekindle my sisterly love, remind me that Toan and I are one. Toan and I already belong to each other: the same blood already flows in our veins. What difference does it make if I give myself to him today? We would only be mingling common blood. I don't ever want to give myself to another man. All men horrify me, repulse me, except for Toan. We gaze at the clouds as they glide silently, serenely past the window. I describe them to Toan, the colors, how the horizon fades in the distance. Entwined like this, we share the same shadows. Toan's kiss is long, deep, penetrating, like the night. After that kiss I know we no longer belong to the moral, human world.

The first night we dine in silence. He is seated facing me, his head bent over, concentrating on his bowl of rice. It is raining. Outside, drops of water splash all around. From the ceiling, the lamp casts a dim, cloudy light over the table. I watch it dapple his face with tiny patches, forcing myself not to see scars, but to imagine the light flowering into golden blossoms. He eats laboriously. We both wait for the other to speak. Toan's hand crawls across the tablecloth, searching for mine. Our fingers open, cross, our hands throbbing with emotion, with desire for each other. Toan stays silent, his head bowed, but I hear him through his touching. After dinner, he takes my hand, leads me to his room.

We stand side by side in the shadows. The light from the street lamp outside, refracted in the rain, illuminates the room, scattering into glistening shards on Toan's body. I let him undress me. His hands are nimble, intelligent. He undoes the buttons one by one, kisses my skin with each measure that he frees it. As he lifts off my bra, lightning flashes through the room, exposing his face. I shudder, glimpsing in the electric blue flash another kind of light, cold and metallic, the blinding slash of a machete. And other machetes spring forth, thunder down, lacerate, hacking away at Toan's face. Through the lightning flashes, through the storm, I see my own body, writhing, appearing and disappearing, shattered images engraved on the warped screen of Toan's face.

"Stop!"

I pull back, terrified.

Sensing my confusion, he draws me into his arms, sending the warmth of his body through mine. He whispers love in my ear, infinite love. "I love you. I don't regret anything. Don't look at my face, it scares you."

He tells me to turn around, not to be afraid anymore, to forget, not to think anymore, to live for us, only us, just him and me. I nod, promise to forget. . . . He comes closer, encircling me in his arms, pressing his body down on my back. The patter of rain against the window pane, Toan's tender, murmuring voice asking if he can enter me from behind, my own voice telling him yes, I need him, give him everything. And then all there is left here, in the apartment, are two beings who love each other.

When he blindfolds me with the black veil he used the other day, the warmth of his body penetrates me, swirls inside me. Through the black veil I saw us clearly: our two naked bodies entwined into one, Toan's arms clasped around my waist, his mouth on the nape of my neck, dropping to my shoulders, biting my back. Welling up from the deepest part in my being, a long, shuddering tenderness rises and spreads through my body. Cradled in the slow, tender rocking of his body, all the pain, the wounds of the past, melt into the startling happiness of this fraternal love.

Toan and I loved each other in the shadow of the night; through the healing tenderness of caresses we helped each other efface our unhappy past. Afterward Toan led me to bed. I slumped onto his chest, wept from happiness that we had compensated each other. My tears spilled over, trickled hot onto his chest. He fondled my chin, asked me if I loved him, if I was happy, if I regretted this.

And I told him that I loved him, that I was happy, that I didn't regret anything. This might be sin, but who else but Toan could understand that a drop of shared blood was worth an ocean of a stranger's? Who would ever understand how much I needed Toan, this drop of my own blood?

The moon rose. The rain stopped. We lay next to each other, listening to the silence, the primal night of our origins. Once, in the tribes, brothers and sisters often married. Toan and I, we were just restoring life to what it had once been, at the dawn of mankind. The emptiness of the night shielded me from the gaze of others, from morality. In this night we were all that existed, a brother and sister who loved each other.

The days that followed, the first of our life together, were magical. I was everything for Toan: elder sister, younger sister, lover, wife. And he was all for me, at once little brother, lover, husband. What awe when feelings merge, when one loves. I couldn't bear being apart from him. Hours spent at the office weighed on me, heavy with longing. I would almost run home, yearning to hold him, to melt into his arms. Feverish kisses, passionate embraces. At night, on my pillow, Toan liked to recall our shared memories.

"Remember our walks, at night, on the beach behind Vung Tau? I'll never forget your violet *ao dai* against the yellow sand that stretched all the way to the foot of the mountains. Back then your hair came all the way down your back, and the wind kept time with the clouds. I've loved you ever since. Did you know?''

Did you know? His face buried in my hair, he murmurs to me, rubs his nose at the nape of my neck. In these moments we relive the past, a time when he still had a normal nose, when I still had the long hair of a girl who hasn't yet been drowned in shame. And Toan stirred many other memories in me; his eyes, blind to present and future, could see only images of the past.

''Remember the first time you put on makeup? For Thuan's birthday party? Niem brought over face powder. . . . I hid behind the door. Maybe you didn't know it. That night papa locked you in your room, forbade you to go out. You cried all night. That made me cry too, remember?''

Remember? Yes, I remember. How you were always clinging to me, how you demanded affection, followed me like a shadow, never leaving me for a second. How you used to refuse to sleep alone, how you sulked whenever Thuan went on walks with me.

''You still love him, don't you?''

Jealous, bitter, he often plied me with questions.

''He kissed you, didn't he? What else did he do with you?''

If I didn't answer, he would be furious, making love to me violently, clawing my back with his nails, as if to take revenge. Afterward, he would weep and beg me to forgive him. If I shook my head, insisting that Thuan was just a friend, he would be reassured that I belonged only to him, as he wished it.

"Promise me. That you'll be with no one but me."

And I would promise, knowing that I could never leave him, never live apart from him.

We hugged each other, took refuge in the shared heat of our bodies, took refuge from the snow falling in drifts outside. Snowflakes gathered on the windowsill, freezing and melting, and freezing again. All winter we hid ourselves in the apartment, avoided the world. I feared our love would be discovered; Toan feared I would abandon him. We could sleep together for hours and hours on end, nestled in the warmth of the covers.

After making love, after I gave myself to him, I would see it floating on the ceiling. The word. *Incest.* I would hide my head in his shoulder, fleeing this invisible word that was nevertheless large and clear on the ceiling.

A black veil over the eyes was the best way for me to stop seeing it. Sometimes, on the weekends, I kept it on all day, sharing Toan's world without light. We played hide-and-seek in the apartment. Hidden behind a door, an armoire, we held our breath. . . . Toan gave me my first lessons in this world of the blind. How do you walk in the dark? How many steps between the kitchen and the living room? How many arm lengths between the table and the television? How do you know when food is cooked?

"By tasting it!"

He would burst out laughing when I asked him that question.

"If you want to keep track of time, know whether it is day or night, you have to learn how to keep track of your own hunger, digestion."

"But how do you choose exactly which clothes to wear?"

"You must learn to feel the fabric, to give a scent to each article of clothing. . . ."

Little by little I learned, entering with delight into this shadowy world. Every time I tripped, he burst out laughing. Whenever he confused wheat flour with corn flour, I giggled, mocking him. I had begun to grasp these brief moments of happiness, begun to understand them, to share them with Toan, ever since we became husband and wife.

I had never known such happiness. The happiness of being a normal woman, of living as a couple. It was a kind of happiness that, ever since the events, I thought I had lost forever. Toan began to attend a school for the blind, and he brought work home to help me out financially. Miserable as these jobs were, the extra money was a joy for us. Toan was happy; he felt useful. I was happy to see him lead a less abnormal life, to see him work at his cello playing, to see him studying French in Braille. He gave up drinking and smoking. This moved me; I realized that he was trying to become a model husband. Sometimes he would stammer like a child, trying to avoid the words . . . *Elder sister.*

"Do you still love me?"

"Always. But only if you still call me Elder sister."

"Why won't you let me call you by your name?"

"I love you, so I always want to be your Elder sister, understand?"

He would nod and fall silent, let me stroke the locks of hair across his forehead. Sometimes, on moonlit nights, we went for walks. Each time I would dress up, and carefully apply my makeup, so he would know I had made myself beautiful for him, so that he would be proud to walk by my side.

Considerate, sensitive, he would always wait for me to change my clothes. When he sensed I was finished, he would tell me, with a serious air, how beautiful I was, seem to gaze at me passionately. Poor Toan. These moments pained me; when his fingers touched my lips, trying to guess the color of my lipstick, when he felt the fabric of my clothes to guess what I was wearing.

"You're beautiful tonight. I'm so happy."

At these moments I felt like crying, but I restrained myself, so as not to ruin the evening. I adjusted his tie, and we went out. Usually Toan took my hand, slipped it in his coat pocket. We took deserted back alleys so that Toan wouldn't hear the murmurs of passersby, the children's frightened shrieks. We have a favorite restaurant near the apartment. We dare go only on Mondays, when it's nearly empty. The old man who owns the restaurant always reserves a table for me in a corner, with a candle and a rose.

"Don't order anything expensive. I only want to be here with you. The food doesn't matter."

We dine in the tender candlelight, the rose slowly opening; the old man is attentive.

"Did you like the meal?"

"Oh, yes, it was perfect," Toan would answer for me, happy, contented. Under the table, all through dinner, our legs entwined.

Winter passes, our love still shrouded in secrecy. Spring comes, prying open the yellow flower buds on the chestnut trees, their skinny branches outstretched like the arms of young girls, weave wreaths of flowers and fruit. Green buds grope forth like we search for life. For a moment, in this dappled, rippling sunlight, in this wondrous nature, I am reborn. I fall back to earth when Toan demands that I give him a child. . . .

I refuse, horrified. The idea of having a child with Toan stabs me, rips away the black veil. I ask Toan: What would we say to our parents, our relatives? We can't live in seclusion, in hiding, for our whole lives. Children conceived in incest are often abnormal. I am terrified. Every time he mentions his desire to have a child, I shudder.

"Don't think about that anymore. It scares me," I say, panic-stricken.

Toan moans, begs, grabs me violently by the waist.

"Give me a child, just one. Someone to call us papa, mama. We'll give it so much love."

Night after night he begs me, insistent, frenzied, oblivious. I have bent my mind to love him, but I don't have the courage to give our crime a human shape. How would we explain our relationship to the child, the relationship between its parents?

"No! I don't want to! We aren't husband and wife, please understand me!" I cry as he covers my neck with kisses.

"But I want one, I want one!" he shouts, shaking his head, stubborn, selfish. My tears are choked, bitter.

"Please, have pity on me, please!" I beg him.

Toan doesn't understand, doesn't realize that I have reached the extreme limits of sisterly love. He just thinks I am rejecting him. From that day on, his attitude toward me changes; he retreats into his shadowy silence, into his old violence. Slowly, imperceptibly, he is transformed, becomes domineering, imperious, mean. He forbids me to take my pill. Obsessed by the desire to force me to have a child, he searches the apartment, discovers all my hiding places. At night I don't dare sleep with him anymore. During the day I drown myself in the television to avoid talking. I live on the defensive, tracked, stalked, waiting for the assault.

The night it happened, I was watching an old film. Disparate images flickered past my eyes, appeared and disappeared. The whine of Toan's cello that had echoed through the apartment resumed its old refrain, tuneless voice, unfeeling, soulless, and it wrapped around my brain like barbed wire. This shrill, razor-sharp sound, like a sliver of glass ripping through flesh, while on the screen I watched the turbulent story. I remember the film had an odd name, *Gunboat on the Yangtze*, Steve McQueen acting the part of a sailor on an American warship in China ferrying between Hankou and Hangzhou. There are certain violent changes in the human mind that are truly horrible, certain instinctive, abnormal reactions. That's all I remember. The rest, the other images, weren't from the film, but of a fetus growing in its mother's body. I saw it on the screen, the uterus bursting, the umbilical cord dangling, the syringes, the body that pushed, and pushed, blood gushing forth with each contraction. And in the surge of blood, a tiny, pointed skull that drew back, reluctant. In the middle of the gaping, bloody uterus, a baby's skull with Steve McQueen's face, lips twisted, eyes rolled back, just like at the end of the film, when the actor falls, struck by a bullet, and then raises himself to his feet, staggering, then crawling through the sticky, viscous liquid. His terrified, distraught eyes fix on the hole in his stomach, the blood gushing forth from it. I hear the last words of a dying man. *"But, but, my God! What has happened to me! Just yesterday I was still at home!"* The baby struggles, fingers scratching, legs kicking the air. The mother's womb splits open, the mad screech of Toan's cello grates on my raw nerves. My head spins with a jumble of sounds and images that couple and merge. I can't understand the sailor's last words. I want to understand, want to see the child's real face, but now, after the flood, the cello falls silent. No more music, just sounds of glass bottles smashing, a door slamming, blood ebbing, a heart that stops beating, lungs that gasp for breath, a uterus closing. Toan stands behind me, motionless.

"Give me a child."

"No! I can't."

He isn't listening. In a blue flash he brandishes a razor blade against my face. Suddenly he slashes a cello string. One. He groans, then picks up the razor blade again, waving it in the air like the black veil, uncertain. The vision of a snake's body coiling around my neck comes back to me as Toan presses the blade to my neck and, gently, cuts. I feel the heat of my blood trickling. Paralyzed, terrified, I struggle with him, my hands scraping the air.

"Stop!"

"You don't love me."

"But I do."

"That's a lie. If you love me, why do you refuse to have my child?" he screams. Then he slashes another cello string. Two.

"No! Please, don't force me!" I push him away, push him over, and flee. He pursues me. The bookcase, the table, the stools—everything topples under me. I trip and fall, pull myself up, fall again; the flower pot trips me, the door blocks my way, now down the long, endless corridor. The bathroom, the bathroom, bolt the door, my father's name, my mother's name, I shout them in answer to Toan's furious blows against the door.

"Oh, God! Leave me alone."

Toan doesn't hear me. He pushes down the door and jumps on me, rips my shirt.

"No! Let go of me!"

I fall onto the tile floor. Toan falls on top of me.

"I'm a cripple. Sometimes I'm crazy, sometimes I'm sane. Is that what scares you, Elder sister? Is that it? You're afraid the child will look like me, is that it? Say it!"

He slaps me, tears off my shirt. His fingers twist my arm, his thighs crush my legs, panting and screaming, the floor, the walls, the ceiling, the towels, naked, clammy bodies, shoulders, muscles taut, a brute force that bites, scratches, pierces, the nose, those eyes, the scars, the semen, the fetus, the child. I scream for my mother. Toan gags me, smothering my voice with his hand.

"Say it! Say you love me, that you want my child. Say it! Say it!"

Toan raped me on the bathroom floor. He said he was hungry for my sweet-smelling flesh, for my firm breasts, my fresh white thighs, for a child, a lively, handsome one. He talked on and on, without stopping, while I thrashed, sobbed, shouted and begged. While I suffered.

I lay naked on the floor, lay there in the bathroom, my senses scattered, haunted by an idea that I couldn't articulate, blood trickling down my lip. All of a sudden the film came back to me, slowly but clearly. I just lay there, replaying the film in my memory. The fight between the marine and his comrades. The captain's moral struggle. The fanatical Chinese. The violent uprising. The assistant mechanic being tortured. The young, naive woman missionary. The bullet that shot through Steve McQueen's stomach and out his back, the words gushing forth at the end, near death. What were they? What did he mean? I couldn't understand them. As if I were watching a silent film.

After a long time I get up; it's daylight out. Toan is slumped on the dining room table, sobbing. Slow, innocent moans. The way he once cried as a little boy. The window is ajar. There's no sun out. I gaze at the murky, clouded sky.

All at once I remember everything, each detail. The moment I got on the boat to cross the sea, to leave my country, the pirates' attacks, everything up to the moment that Toan raped me. . . .

I remember every one of the wounded sailor's last words. *But, but . . . My God, what happened? Just yesterday we were still in Vung Tau!* I collapse. Toan turns his ravaged face toward me. Scars.

My God, it's daylight.

THE BACK STREETS
OF HOI AN

Returning to live in Hoi An, Loan had fallen under the
spell of Lu's charm. Lady Thi, who had rented her a
room in her house on Moss Street, told anyone who
was willing to listen that Loan had been bewitched.
Everything had started the day Lu took her to visit the
Cau Nhat pagoda. Beneath the dirty walls and sagging
roof, he invited Loan to listen to the echo of the centuries of history that wandered between the walls. She
remembered staring, petrified, at the two statues of the
Di Lac Buddha, their pockmarked faces, their broken

noses. A chipped elbow, a foot missing some toes. Next to them, gnawed away by time, stood the statues of Good and Evil. The pagoda seemed to have laid in wait for Loan, waited to reveal the sadness of an era, an entire culture. Amidst the deserted silence of the ruins, Lu's voice was the only living sound. Lu exhaled the smoke of his cigarette, whispering in her ear. His hypnotic, relentless voice recounted the past, his hand insistently caressing Loan's wrist, as if it were the link in a chain that would bind them forever. Loan shuddered in terror. This illicit love terrified her. And yet she gave herself to it, utterly. She was ruthless to her husband and daughter. For a long time afterward, every time she remembered it, she was tortured by remorse and shame, and silently she prayed for her husband's forgiveness.

Thinking back on the town of Hoi An rarely reminded her of Dan's face, or that of her daughter, Hanh. All she could see was the slanting saffron light that flickered down the shadowy streets, down the sidewalks, swaying over the barren tips of the coconut trees, their wizened, scraggly roots. Hoi An, just a small provincial town in central Vietnam, but its snaking rows of streets had been carved into Loan's memory as finely as mother-of-pearl under a sculptor's knife. The three-pavilion houses encircling a courtyard, the jagged rooftops, rippling like waves, as far as the eye could see, the arched gateways, the doors of bamboo slats, the silence. . . . You had to have lived there, under the blistering heat at noon, in Lady Thi's courtyard, heard the deafening silence filter through the earth and the rocks, listened to the distant creak of the wooden pillars. You had to have heard each crack of the lime whitewash the length of the ancient walls, to have watched the odd, sinister drip of the thick light that sweated from the sky, to understand Hoi An's tragedy.

A dead town, never to be revived. Not by the rainy season, not by the dry season. Lu used to say that once, during the rainy season, the Thu Bon River had been covered with junks and boats. Today, all that's left is the glitter of the murky waters, the mournful reflection of a town forgotten between two pages of history. It was on the way back from the Cau Nhat pagoda that Loan grasped the rhythm of Hoi An for the first time, in the padding footsteps of children, in the howl of their laughter coiling down the narrow back streets, exploding in the silence. A silence that made you shiver. A hundred years ago, Lu says Moss Street was prosperous, bustling. Now it was like a corpse someone had laid out but forgotten to bury.

Lu brings Loan back to Lady Thi's place, pulls her toward the hammock suspended in the courtyard, seats her on his thighs, swings her there. Shy, distracted, Loan realizes with surprise that with him she is submissive, totally obedient. What just happened between them, in the courtyard behind the pagoda, makes Loan shudder; she tries to forget. At her age, she is no longer a girl, but to dare such obscenities, on such sacred ground. Lu doesn't give her time to think; he takes her hand, points at the ceramic tiles on the rooftops opposite. Drenched in the sun, glistening, the tubular tiles seem to dance, row after row, a vast sea of incandescent brass. A sea crested with dancing tiles, wave after rippling wave, rooftop after rooftop, endless.

Lu says that each tile represents a decade. Each a decade in the ancient history of Hoi An, back when it was still called Hai Pho, or "Ocean Boulevard," with the mouth of the Dai Chiem River that opened onto the sea, back when the warlords invaded, massacred. Lu recounted, passionate, breathless, the slaughter that had taken place in Hoi An. Loan clung to his neck, terrified. All of Lu's stories ended in blood. The very spot where Loan had nestled in Lu's arms had been an execution ground. Suddenly Loan pitches forward, but her head lurches back, yanked by Lu's hand. He drags her by the hair, grips Loan in his arms like the Cham once held the Sa Huynh, or the way the Vietnamese once gripped the Cham before beheading them. Lu tells Loan to throw her head back so he can kiss her lips, bite her neck. Her heart races as Lu greedily sucks at the skin on her neck, as his teeth paint her neck violet, the dark bloody chicken liver color of the high, moss-covered stone walls surrounding Lady Thi's house. Loan shuddered, remembering. The story of her adultery had just begun.

The sun is a bottomless inferno in the silence of the afternoon. Fierce, violent sun of the dry, sandy shores.

Sun that stings the eyes, that parches and numbs, that lashes the throat. Loan feels as if she is on a bed of smoldering coals. On those afternoons, seated at Lu's side in Lady Thi's living room, she is like a madwoman, infatuated, dazed, as if she has cast off the anchors of time of plunge into another era. Loan only comes to her senses each time she hears Lady Thi order the servant in a low voice to serve tea. Tea cascades into Loan's cup, clacking, splattering, scalding her feverish body, flowing like a river of lava through her body. Loan looks up, furious, flashes the girl a threatening look. The servant looks away, narrowing her eyes to slits. More tea, a slow trickle that fills the cup. Loan stares at the two cups, the shiver of the dark red tea leaves. Lu watches the scene in silence, releases his grip on Loan's body, takes a drag on his cigarette, flicking the ash into an old earthenware bowl, as wide as an urn, like the crimson mouth of an old crone chewing a betel quid. Cigarette smoke swirls around Lu's face, dense, yellow-brown, like the color of scorched earth. Lu laughs with his eyes, sneering at Loan's exasperation. The servant turns to leave. But Lu orders her to make more tea. She hammers the ground with her clogs as she walks away. So the girl must hate her? Out of jealousy? Anger? Could she too be in love with Lu? An insidious hostility that Loan doesn't understand, only hears in the pounding thud of the girl's clogs, like the blows of butchers' cleavers on the day of a funeral banquet. The click-clack of the clogs fades, then stops.

Only when the girl's silhouette has vanished into the dark frame of an old door does Lu snuff out his cigarette, strangling the butt as if he were crushing an animal to death under his fingers. In this man's gesture Loan sees the flicker of an extraordinary brutality that both attracts and repels her. Lu gazes at Loan, slowly unfurls his hand, the left hand, the one that wears the ring, with the sharp nails, the rough fingers. Lu tells Loan to pull up her shirt, he wants to stroke the length of her spine. Loan starts, as if pins were pricking her back. Lu rubs, whittles, paints, and pierces, as concentrated as a sculptor. Loan shudders with pleasure and fear; the sense that she is being watched only arouses, sharpens her desire. Is that the glow of Lady Thi's eyes peering at them through a crack in the wall? Or the piercing gaze, as thin as a hair, of the servant crouched down, hiding behind the door? Her shoulders hunched up high, her eyes shut, Loan loses herself in the sweet pain of Lu's nails clawing, scraping her back.

Still caressing her, Lu recounts the massacre of the Sa Huynh people. As if possessed, he describes every detail of the murders, the decapitations, the women raped, then burned alive. His voice flows naturally, his fingers reaping one by one the wild, chaotic pulsing of her veins, the shivers, her choked gasps, the panting, greedy, impatient, desperate, shameful moans of desire. Loan's heart pounds as she listens to history flow from Lu's regular voice, as it moves from one bloody, barbarous era to the next. His eyes, those eyes that everyone finds black with indifference, are half-closed, glinting softly in the expectancy of pleasure, opening only when the dry heat of the afternoon has scorched away all the demands of the flesh. Only then does she feel sated, as if she had just made love with him.

Loan's heartbeat slows now; the courtyard paved with stone tiles falls back into the mute silence of history. When it passed through Hoi An, history only left mournful traces. Day by day Loan becomes more and more obsessed by the pages of history written in the blood of the Cham and the Sa Huynh peoples. Is it Lu's mesmeric voice? He has an uncanny way of captivating Loan, like a historian tracking the fault lines of a society whose ancient foundations have crumbled, that teeters on the edge of disintegration. In the beginning she tried to resist, but as Lu once said to her: No one resists time. Little by little, in the silence of those deserted afternoons in Lady Thi's courtyard, Loan felt a fire spread through her body, the same fire that trickled down in from the wavy rooftops, like this love story that she had seen written in the ruins of dead civilization, and which now shot forth, consuming her. Loan loved Lu. Rather, Loan was bewitched by Lu.

Loan married at twenty-six. At thirty-one she had followed her husband, Dan, to live in Hoi An. Their daughter, Hanh, born a year before their marriage, came with them to Lady Thi's place. Every time she came face to face with Lady Thi, Loan wondered how this middle-aged woman managed to live in this world of feudal tradition that welled up from the depths of past centuries. Even the noble title "Lady" refused to deliver her, despite all the vicissitudes, the insane tumult, that had ravaged this place.

Lady Thi had an odd way of serving tea. When she poured, she lifted the teapot, letting the jet of tea splatter as it fell into the brown earthenware cups. Elsewhere, this little tic might have gone unnoticed amidst other idiosyncrasies. But here, on Moss Street, under the sullen, motionless sky, in the deadly quiet where the batting of a fly's wing was enough to provoke pandemonium, Lady Thi's mannered pouring, the hollow spatter of the tea, echoed in mute defiance. Deep contempt. Implacable pettiness. A challenge. Naturally, Loan was the object of this contempt. At first, when she had come to live here, she had just smiled, a modest smile she knew was terribly seductive. But the way Lu chatted familiarly with Lady Thi, as if he were her son or nephew, irritated Loan. She showed her irritation in the way she reached for the tea, taking a cup of it, negligently, from Lady Thi, as if from the hands of a servant. She didn't thank her, just smirked slightly, as if to say *That's enough, leave it!* Then, as soon as Lady Thi had turned her back, incapable of restraining herself, Loan would drain her cup in single gulp and then spit violently onto the courtyard. She wasn't spitting out the tea; she was spitting the putrid phlegm of her sick lungs. Hearing the noise, Lady Thi turned and, ever so slightly, shot Loan a threatening look.

A blue fly landed, nonchalantly, on the edge of the table. Loan fiddled with her cup, a mocking gesture, as if to say: *Ah, more tea? More of the ritual pouring?* Her back was turned, but she still felt Lady Thi's look pierce her half-closed eyelids, shoot straight down her spine. At the bottom of her cup, Loan saw her satisfied smile reflected in the mirror of the tea stain. Satisfied, like after lovemaking with Lu. And suddenly, Loan felt the need to confront Lady Thi, to look this livid face of the past in the eye. Lady Thi was seated on the low wooden bed, hugging her knees, motionless. The mat she slept on was threadbare, tatty, ripped in spots, an odd contrast to her impeccably pressed clothes. The smooth, unctuous silk of her blouse clashed with her severe, tightly bound chignon. Her smoky black eyes stood out against the milky coconut white silk. Lady Thi's nose was as sharp as the back of a knife, her mouth as pointy as a barnacle, her face as narrow as if it had been compressed, on the verge of exploding. Lady Thi fixed her smoky eyes on Loan's face with the precision of an acupuncturist searching for a neural point. The look of a tripe monger supervising the butchering of a pig. Loan felt as if her body were on fire; this battle would take place on this very ground, inside these four smoke-blackened walls. No physical contact, only looks, lightning flashes ripping through the air, ruthless, unending blows.

Lady Thi stared at her, indignant, as if she were glaring at a duck whose neck she had just wrung but that still scurried, insolent, around the courtyard. Loan's eyes were no less murderous; she had studied the gaze of the buffalo butchers, powerful, sharper than Lu's hatchet. Loan took up the challenge and stared back into Lady Thi's eyes, then slowly shifted her gaze from the quivering wings of a bluefly buzzing at the edge of the table, down to the foot of the chair, tracked a blood-red stain of betel spittle drying on the dirt floor, climbed into the wooden clogs under the bed, grazed the surface of the bed, rising to fix, motionless, implacable, on the goiter in the middle of Lady Thi's neck.

Loan stared at it, as she would gape at a leper, as if she were ferreting with a drill the coarse skin speckled with ashen age spots. She could see Thi's body tense, the veins of her goiter quiver, retract, tighten and contort, ready to snap. The goiter was Lady Thi's true face. The longer Loan observed it, the more clearly she distilled in it all the secret cruelty of this wizened, twisted, desiccated woman. The more the goiter swelled, the smaller Lady Thi's face shrank. When she moved, the goiter swung from side to side, as if nostalgic, straining to catch the scent of time past. When Lady Thi sat down, the goiter began to pulsate, as if writhing under Loan's contemptuous gaze. Scarlet now, the pulsating, tiny veins swelled; the goiter struggled like a fetus in the belly of a woman on the verge of childbirth. Loan continued to bore her gaze into the goiter, until, gorged with rage, it became epileptic, thrashing in indecent jerks, ready to burst and ooze onto the floor.

But Lady Thi couldn't stand it; she stood up, coughed dryly, and shuffled off, clacking her clogs against the floor. All that was left on the bed was a teapot full of cold tea, an empty earthenware cup, tea leaves, a moist film of sweat that refused to evaporate. The echo of the past flickered out under Lady Thi's footsteps, the clicking, chaotic swish of the bamboo curtain. When the slats of the curtain lay still, Lady Thi's shadow disappeared into a crevice gnawed by termites in the middle of the house. Loan clucked her tongue, sorry to have missed the spectacle.

Loan flexed her legs, slipped on her sandals, got up, and went into her room. Her room, so to speak, since it was only a partition off a corridor that looked directly out onto the street. Loan and her husband had rented the middle of the house; Lady Thi lived in a room to the left that doubled as a living room, and Lu in a room to the right. The houses in Hoi An were riddled with tiny, circular windows. Every day, through one of them, like a porthole in the stone wall, Loan watched Dan leave the house. His car cluttered the street, blocked traffic. Children chased after it until it disappeared from sight. All the houses on Moss Street had doors that opened onto two parallel streets. Loan saw Dan off at the front door, and waited for Lu's arrival at the back. He always came around noon—you could hear him slam the breaks on his bicycle some ten yards away. She would never forget his face when he crossed the courtyard, stopping in front of her door. He would be there, his face taut, his skin tanned, furrowed with wrinkles; and he would look at her with those wild, mesmerizing eyes that overwhelmed her, heart and soul. As soon as he looked at her, Loan felt her body go limp, ready to do anything he asked. Lu wielded his eyes the way a murderer uses a knife; he knew just where to plunge it to draw the most blood, where to cut, or stab to stop a throat from crying out. In her staring matches with Lady Thi, Loan had mastered only a fraction of Lu's art. Each time she found herself face to face with Lu, she felt as if she were stretching her neck toward the blade of a knife.

But Lu never came in immediately, never spoke to her right away. He always kept her waiting. An infinite, almost unbearable moment. Unfathomable. Terrifying. Loan shot a glance toward the screen that separated their two rooms, vigilant, expectant, sensing the faintest sound from Lu's body. Like a cat lying in wait for a mouse, she recoiled, her eyes glinting, ears pricked, claws kneading the mat. In Lu's room she could hear the padding of sandals, the creak of a chair, the snap of a newspaper opening and closing, the gurgle of water down a pipe. When she heard the rustle of fabric, she imagined Lu undressing, pulling off his ragged khaki shirt and putting on a short-sleeved one. An old shirt, a bright blue, almost turquoise, with two epaulettes, two pockets, missing a button. The one he had worn the day they went to the Cau Nhat pagoda. The one she had nuzzled against when she noticed, through a hole in the fabric, how his tanned skin dipped at the belly button, which was as deep as a well, with a few hairs and a beauty mark right above the belt. Every time she thought of it, she broke into a sweat. And suddenly she would become impatient, brutal. She shouted at the servant, ordering her to go look for Hanh. She would scream and shriek, barely able to restrain herself from giving the girl a slap when she was slow to execute. Even after the servant had left, Loan could still see the beauty mark floating on the panel, the hairs quivering, bending and straightening, mocking. The idea that she couldn't touch them tortured her. Was he cruel enough to leave her? The heavy, cloying, nauseating smell of the incense that Lady Thi burned to honor the memory of Long Chu flooded into Loan's room, as if to remind her of the obscene way she had given herself to Lu in the courtyard of the Cau Nhat pagoda. Loan remembered every detail: the old stand of bamboo near the two jars of water; the wooden statue of a dog that replaced one the floods had carried away the previous year; the flecks of ash that slowly fell from the sticks of incense stuck in the earthenware bowls; the flickering glow of the saffron robes the Buddhist nuns wore when they came to sound the gong, which echoed the hollow *clap-clap* of the tiny wooden hand drum, which beat in rhythm to Lu's sharp, bloody nails as they kneaded her flesh. One of Lu's hands was misshapen, with a large, flat thumbnail, and a huge index finger, yellowed by cigarette smoke, deft, accusatory.

Loan gripped the hem of her pants, pulling them taut against her legs; they were slick with sweat, as if drenched in grease. The veins in her wrists were greenish, swollen. The sleeves of her blouse were also sodden with the sweat that streamed down the palms of her hands. Loan bent over, wiping them on her knees. The thin partition that separated her room from Lu's seemed to mock her. Her nerves were raw, as if paralyzed by an electric shock; her temples pounded, her head felt as if it would explode. The urge to destroy overcame her, to smash, break, and burn everything—mosquito net, covers, books, notebooks, cups, bowls, vases, flasks. She yearned to plunge into Lu's room, to scream: *You bastard!* Just when she least expected it, as she sank into delirium, Lu appeared, passed outside her door, shot her an imperious look. Just a flash of a look and then left. Loan followed him in silence, lost.

They strolled all the way down Moss Street, passed under a low wooden gate next to a sagging, sparse coconut tree. The dried-out trunk, eaten away by termites, was weblike, as if it had been woven out of thread. Sunlight trickled off a telephone pole, zigzagging down streets as narrow and tangled as the lines of a hand.

Lu led Loan to the banks of the Thu Bon River. The surface of the water shivered. The river was deserted, except for a few old barges. The scorching August sun beat down, drying out even the rinds of the fruit on the citrus trees. Loan felt her skin sizzle, and she flushed when Lu took her hand and began to tell her about the water festivals on the Thu Bon. Loan listened, rapt, as Lu described the rites and customs: the prayers to heaven and earth; how they built the papier-mâché funeral effigy of Long Chu; the way the painter dabbed the eyes of the statue on with a brush; how a Buddhist priest clad in a toga with a Ti Lu miter had once summoned the spirit of Chu Long with a magic wand. Then the processions, the kowtowing, more prayers, the cremation, and the slow drift of the flaming body down the river. . . . Lu's hypnotic voice seeped into Loan's soul, drawing her into a world of mystery and superstition. Lu told it again, one more time, the carnage of history that had taken place on the banks of this river that flowed beneath their eyes, the wars between the Cham and the Sa Huynh, and then between the Cham and the Viets. A bloodred stain slowly spread on the glistening, sunlit water. A clamor of arms rose suddenly from the sterile bowels of the earth. Bodies clashed, tore at each other and fell, clogging the river. And then Lu stopped, leaving Loan's body to steep in the tales of these ancient savageries. He returned from the market with a basket of anchovies, still flicking and twisting in the net, oozing and slimy between his fingers.

"Eat!"

He ripped the head off a fish and stuffed it in Loan's mouth. He fed her meticulously, mouthful by mouthful, waiting patiently until she had swallowed each piece before presenting the next. The fish had a nauseating flavor. As Loan crushed each fish's stomach between her teeth, a bitter taste would suddenly flood into her mouth. Lu kept ripping the heads off the fish, stuffing the meat into her mouth. Fish blood trickled over her chest, titillating her senses, kindling her desire. Feverishly, Loan sucked Lu's fingers, the salty blood dripping, drop by drop, onto the front of her blouse. The blazing, torrid sun beat down on her head, making her feel dizzy. Loan knew that fishermen had flocked around them to gape at her, but she couldn't tear herself away from Lu's fiendish hands, or resist him. But was it Lu? Or the superstitious ceremonies of Hoi An? The barbaric lure of history? The fish, still alive, struggled in her mouth, attacked her tongue, darted between her teeth, biting the inside of her lips, choking her. Hunched over, moaning, Loan suddenly jerked her head away. But Lu grabbed her neck and pressed her head back down into the basket of fish. Lu's movement as he pushed fish into Loan's mouth, and her movement, gasping for breath before plunging again, were so syncopated that Loan could see their shadows coupling on the ground. Every time she was able to bite one of Lu's fingers, she felt satisfied. Her eyes, nostrils, and mouth were slick with the slime and scales of the fish. And she ate, bewitched, to the very end, until there were no more. The last fish swallowed, Lu took her back to Lady Thi's place.

Green betel leaves had been laid out on the smooth, polished surface of the black wooden bed. Lady Thi cut an areca nut in two, daubed a betel leaf with a layer of lime paste, wrapped a slice of the nut in the mixture, and chewed it between her toothless gums. She was crouched down, her knees clutched to her chest, silent. From time to time she flicked her fan to stir the wind. Lady Thi didn't look at Loan, but her goiter dilated with rage, as if to say: *I know everything, in minute detail.* Lu casually sat down on the chair and, without asking, reached for Lady Thi's water pipe. He rolled some tobacco into a ball between his fingers, tamped it into the pipe, and lit it. The water whistled and sputtered. A thick, clammy smoke poured from his flat nostrils, which quivered as they rose and fell in the rhythm of addiction. Lu's face remained expressionless. A thin thread of smoke spread languorously through the room, refusing to dissipate. Loan too reached for the pipe and sucked in the smoke, intoxicating herself on the centuries.

Loan got up, stood motionless for a moment, and then went out into the courtyard to wash her face. The clear water in the washbowl reflected back the image of a woman fulfilled. Sun-warmed water, water from the Thu Bon River; Loan cupped her hands together, scooping some up in her palms, as if straining to capture an enchanted image. She combed her hair and put on a light mauve blouse embroidered with tiny red flowers. When she left her room, the flowers bloomed, radiant in the freshness of the silk. Loan felt happy, her spirit free, her body as light as if she had just stepped out of a bath. She leaned against the door frame, watched Lu chatting with Lady Thi. Lu was telling her about something that had happened in the street. Lady Thi muttered a reply. Loan went out into the courtyard to get a glass of water for Lu. With her back turned, sheltered from Lady Thi's gaze, she couldn't help beaming to herself, basking in a feeling of secret complicity and gratitude toward Lu. She could tell that Lu was laughing to himself too. Both of them, in silence, his deep laugh merging with her woman's laugh, echoing through the house. Suddenly she felt girlish, vulnerable. As if she were in love for the first time. Their joyous, mischievous laughter spread soundlessly through her body. Loan glanced discreetly, playfully, at Lu before going into the other room. But she didn't go all the way in. Surreptitiously, from behind the bamboo curtain, she continued to watch him. Lady Thi asked Lu in a listless voice about the funeral of a neighbor who had lived down the street. He responded vaguely, his finger caressing the edge of his glass. He took the flask of the water pipe in his hand, turning it back and forth, squeezing it and releasing it, pulling it toward him and pushing it away. Again, Loan felt desire rise in her, the yearning to press her face against Lu's rough, hard palm, to suck one by one his seawater-puckered fingers, to lick one by one his sharp nails, the thin crusts of dirt that lay under them. Loan remained lost in thought, thinking of those hands, until little Hanh called out to her: "Mama, are you home? Is dinner ready yet?" She ordered the servant to set the table and serve the meal, a thick soup, tofu sautéed in lard. Flies scattered when she lifted the cover off the tray to reveal a small pot of cold, burned rice.

Dan was a mature, dependable man. Mature, like a bamboo pole, stiff, oblivious. Dan liked to take care of his wife, dote on her. Perhaps Loan had married him for his quality. But as time went by, she discovered that it wasn't enough for her, that something in their relationship was lacking. And this lack was clear to Loan when she gave herself to Lu. Lu's shoulder was hard, gave off a powerful earthy salt smell. Dan's was fat, soft, tasteless. Nevertheless, the two men bore a strange resemblance to each other in one way: they were both passionate about history. Dan had moved Loan and Hanh to live in Hoi An solely to pursue his research. The first few weeks after their arrival, she had accompanied Dan on digs at various archeological sites. Ancient wells buried under layers of sand, antique tombs that dated back to nobody knew when, or who had built them.

The only thing the digs uncovered, as far as Loan could see, was earth. In certain places it was dark red, as if it had been steeped in blood; in other places it was a rich, dusty yellow, like tumeric. Different colors, but always the same earth, nothing but earth. Dan dug, sifted, sorting and analyzing, searching for proof of the existence of a Sa Huynh culture. He beamed when he came home at night boasting of the authentic pieces that he had just uncovered that day, and Loan wondered, anxious, if he knew about her affair with Lu. They lived in a tiny provincial town, the kind of place where people noticed a broken roof tile. How could he be oblivious to the scandalous affair between Loan and Lu? Did he not know, or did he already know too much?

Loan read a secret jealousy in the way her servant, Lien, stared, narrowed her eyes, in the way she looked at Dan. Could Lien be jealous of Loan's relationship with Dan? Lien was nineteen, but she had the waist of a fourteen-year-old girl. Dan had hired her to help Loan with housework and take care of Hanh. Both maid and nanny in one, Lien lacked only one quality needed to become the ideal attendant: an understanding of life, and the ability to become Loan's confidant. Lien's slitty eel eyes and overly long hair that slithered, serpent-like, down her back, exasperated Loan. That and her lisping central accent. Loan wanted to fire her, but Dan refused, praising her resourcefulness. Loan didn't know whether Lien was resourceful or not; all she could see was the way the girl eyed Lu on the sly, the look of a female that had never tasted flesh. Loan hated seeing Lien carry Lu's clothes off to be washed.

And yet she was the one who had asked Lien to do this chore. Lien would rub the collars with soap and then, instead of scrubbing them rapidly, would dreamily caress the fabric, running her fingers along the seams, touching the cloth as if she were stroking Lu's body. Whenever Loan surprised her doing this, she would shout at the girl: What are you doing dawdling over this tiny basket of clothes? Are you going to spend the whole day on this? Then Loan would order her to leave the washing and to go do the shopping, reserving for herself the pleasure of washing Lu's clothes, of smelling his sweat, recognizing an old stain. Of fish blood. The pungent odor of Lu's sweat, as if marinated in lemon grass, intoxicated her.

Dan came home evenings for dinner. One evening there was a cloudy mussel soup, thickened with potato starch. Lien brought out a plate of sautéed shrimp, sliced and arranged in arching crescents as fine as a lady's fingernails. Flecks of black pepper floated on a bowl of stewed fish. Dan counted out the chopsticks with gusto, and handed a pair to Lady Thi. Her goiter swung back and forth, nodding in compliance, staring at each of the dishes, as if to memorize their place. Loan was seated between Dan and little Hanh. Give me some fish and shrimp, Mama, Hanh asked sweetly. Loan reached with her chopsticks to tear off a piece of fish. But it slipped from her grasp. Dan came to his wife's rescue. Lifting her head, Loan was surprised to see an ironic smile flicker at the corners of Lu's mouth. His lips were slightly tilted, ajar, revealing a flash of ivory; they pressed together, closing and opening, always mocking. Suddenly Dan's attentiveness irritated Loan. He kept plopping pieces of fish in her bowl. Every time she ate a piece, Loan would give Lu a look, as if to say: *See, I don't want to receive anything more from him.* Lady Thi stared at Loan, hostile, noisily chewing a tough piece of a mussel. Oblivious, Dan continued to recount the discovery of a round, rotating table made of stone, a highly refined example of Sa Huynh art that the dig team had just uncovered. From time to time, as the buzz of horseflies came nearer, Loan would swat them away with the back of her hand. Hanh had barely touched the food on her plate. Loan rose and took her daughter to the kitchen to wash up. Lien was there, eating alone. As soon as she saw Loan, she wheeled around, showing Loan her back covered with her long, flowing hair. When Loan returned to the table, she didn't sit down in her former place; she chose Hanh's, next to Lu.

Under the table, as predicted, Lu's hand came to rest on Loan's thigh, near her crotch, where the flesh was young and tender. Loan felt her body inflamed, a wave of desire breaking over her. She pretended to gaze at Lady Thi's goiter; she smiled sweetly into Dan's un-suspecting face as Lu's fingers sucked like lips at her thigh. She squeezed her knees together, at once furious, anxious, aroused. From the depths of her heart rose a sensation of pride, satisfaction: Lu hadn't been able to restrain himself; he had to touch her body. Loan lifted her bowl, pretending to pick at a grain of rice, and shot Lu a look—half dissuasive, half encouraging. Lu's fingers became more and more daring. Loan froze, straining to remain poised. She felt her spine tense, her shoulders numb. Lu described the three-pointed earrings of Sa Huynh, an ancient form of stone jewelry. The earrings were inserted into the ears permanently and the Sa Huynh women wore them to their grave; they were so heavy they could stretch the earlobes down to the chin. Sometimes the ears ripped, became infected, and had to be cut off. A woman without ears was as ignominious as a woman who had lost her virginity. Dan said that they had found earrings at the bottom of an old well. No doubt left from women who had committed suicide there. For fear of being burned alive on their husband's funeral pyre? Because their ears had become infected? Loan shuddered as Lu's hand slipped toward her stomach; a blade twisted in her gut. Loan laid down her chopsticks, slipped her hand under the tablecloth, and pinched Lu's hand until she drew blood. Lu's fingers unclenched for a moment, then closed again like tentacles over her thigh. And he continued to chat with Dan as if nothing had happened, while his hand, burning, impudent, pressed and stroked, licking the humid flesh of Loan's thighs. Two strong male fingers, the thumb and the index, muscular, rough. Loan almost collapsed, screamed. Pain screwed into her flesh, her hair stood on end, a strange cry stuck in her throat. She felt like twisting free, like begging Lu to stop, but she didn't dare. Lady Thi kept scooping spoonfuls of clear broth onto her rice. Dan took slow, deliberate puffs on the bamboo water pipe. And so life goes on, day after day. As does history, century after century. Dan didn't notice that Loan was twisting in pain. The muscles and nerves of Lu's hand stretched, coiling strength into his two fingers to tear at her skin. The barbaric game dragged on and on, implacable, ruthless, until Loan, unable to stand it any longer, bent over, lips pinched, eyes bloodshot, imploring. Lu's fingers slowly unfurled, let go. Loan was bathed in sweat, limp, as after a violent coupling. There was no one like Loan, no one else who loved, as she did, to tear her gut, who would rip into her own flesh to sate him.

Lunch was over. Lu left on his bicycle, Dan in his car. The streets echoed with the joyful laughter of children. A few climbed onto the trunk of Dan's car, hanging on until the car reached the main road. Lady Thi's house sank back into the immobility of the past. The rooftops slanted toward the ground, pouring shimmering sunlight onto the ground. Little Hanh slept. Seated at the head of her daughter's bed, Loan listened distractedly to the sound of the servant scooping water to fill the washbasin. The water seemed to murmur something; Loan couldn't put a name to it, but it felt full of fury.

Loan fanned Hanh for a while, then stopped. The pain rose again, stinging, burning the tender flesh of her thigh. She rolled up the leg of her pants; the skin was raw, purple where his nails had left deep traces. She gently caressed her thigh, as if to console it. She murmured, her voice half choked, as distant as the broken strains of an ancient lullaby. The crimson skin attracted her, inviting, irresistible. Loan dug her nails into the wounds. She shuddered, cringing under the electric shock of it. Like vinegar poured onto an open wound. But it was also the maddening burn of a wound that was closing, of new skin that begged to be scratched until blood appeared. Loan pulled back her hand, but couldn't stop herself from starting again. Always the same stabbing pain.

Water slapping against the ground in the afternoon silence awakened Loan. The servant girl, Lien, after finishing the dishes, had flung the water from the basin into the courtyard. That sound, the slap of the water, was like a stinging insult in Loan's direction.

With each passing day the love between Loan and Lu grew more twisted, more reckless. Like the history of the Viets at that irresistible moment, in the mid-eleventh century, when in search of new lands they invaded the South and massacred the weaker peoples who lived there. Day by day Loan grew accustomed to Lu's games—sometimes puerile, sometimes furtive, sometimes reckless—to the point that she could no longer live without them. The strange clandestine nature of their lovemaking, half-private, half-public, veiled and yet transparent, discreet yet brazen, utterly confused Loan. Each day she lost a little more self-control; each day she drew nearer to the brink of his challenge. One day, after lunch and Dan's departure, Loan dragged Lu into her room. Never, since the beginning of her adultery, had Loan felt so brazen, so determined, so reckless. She looked Lu straight in the eye, told him she couldn't stand it any longer—Dan's face, Lady Thi's presence. The feeling of constantly being spied on by the servant, as if the public security police were constantly tailing her. She demanded revenge, demanded they make their affair public. Lu stared fixedly at Loan for a long time, weighing her resolve. Lu's lips, still greasy from lunch, smiled without smiling, attentive, ironic. Loan felt like slapping that diabolical look, that danced, mocking on those lips, those lips that had run countless times over her body. She raised her hand. Lu caught it, glaring at her. Instantly Loan fell back, heavy, inert, submissive. Lu opened the door and shouted for the servant girl. She entered the room, and Lu grabbed her by the hair, forcing her to her knees at Loan's feet. Lien went pale, her skin turning sallow, a yellowy, banana-leaf green. She mumbled something incomprehensible. Still holding, the servant by her hair, Lu shoved her pockmarked face toward Loan:

"Hit!"

Terror welled up in Lien's eyes. Years later, thinking back on it, Loan could see the girl's eyes clearly, thin as razors, dilated, the terror brimming, overflowing, swelling her normally flat face until it was as puffy as the scarred, idiotic face of the Di Lac Buddha at the Cau Nhat pagoda. But in this face in front of her, transfixed by fear, shriveled up, and sunk back into the girl's shoulders, Loan could see all the baseness, the vulgarity, the cowardice, of this girl crumpled at Lu's feet, begging for mercy. Loan howled and then hit, as she had never hit anyone in her life, over and over, arms flailing. Then Lu let go so that Loan could beat her as she wished. Lien fell back, her head hitting the ground hard. Her sobbing, in the Quang accent, sounded like grunts rather than tears, and only sharpened Loan's rage; she pummeled Lien's frightened eyes with her fists. Whenever the girl tried to stand up, Loan only slapped harder, pushing her back down, hitting with both hands, scratching, pinching, tearing Lien's clothes into shreds. When she stopped, her hands were streaming with blood. The servant fell onto the floor, inanimate. A swollen, bruised body, like a drowned buffalo.

Lu pulled Loan toward the bed, undressed her. After the beating Loan was ecstatic, transported. As soon as Lu pulled her to the bed, she wrapped herself around him passionately, climaxing immediately, not so much from Lu's body but from the pain that dripped from the servant's body. Loan cried out, screaming Lu, Lu, choked with pleasure, her body numb. She pulled off

Lu's clothes, kissing, biting, sinking her teeth into the brown, tanned skin on his shoulder, sucking the puffy vein on his neck between her teeth as if she were afraid he would retreat and abandon her. Loan's body was drenched in sweat; the midday sun beat down, scalding, sticky. Salty sweat trickled, drop by drop, onto her lips—salty, like the drops of fish blood. Lu dragged Loan onto the bed to lie down, but she resisted, sliding to the floor, pressing her back down on the cool tiles. Through the slits of Lu's fingers stretched over her face, she could see Lien cowering, collapsed in the corner. Lien's hair bristled, like a medium possessed by spirits, her eyes bulged; her clothes were now nothing but rags, her shirt ripped open, a cheap lace bra over her breasts as flat as two squashed fruits. Her eyes, as sharp and as thin as razors, but lucid, were fixed on Lu and Loan. The idea of conquering, of possessing Lu, the sheer intoxication of winning, under the eyes of her servant brought Loan to orgasm. She could no longer scream Lu's name; she was coming, her body jerking, her hair and ears slick with sweat. She grasped Lu's waist between her knees and yet felt as if he were slipping away, escaping her, as if nothing could hold him back. Loan panted, moaning louder and louder as a heat rose within her, as if Lu had thrust burning coals into her stomach.

Long after that afternoon, when Loan remembered Hoi An, she could no longer remember exactly what had happened. She knew only that she lived in that state for a long time. A terra-cotta urn filled with fresh, icy water. A courtyard dappled with sunlight. An open room. Dan's car coming and going, the tapping of his typewriter in the evenings on the only table in the house. Lady Thi's shadow silently swinging; the way her goiter dangled, sometimes shriveled, sometimes puffy with anger. The innocent pitter-patter of Hanh's footsteps running through the house; the pockmarked Buddha face of the servant girl, growing each day more sullen, more amorphous. Lu's games. And Dan, as he tirelessly transcribed history, the noble facts of the dynasties of kings and lords who had reigned over the country. Slowly, with time, Loan understood that there are three kinds of people in life: those who record history, those who are its victims, and . . .

It took her a long time to guess who made up the third.

NHA NAM

We return to Nha Nam, Th's homeland, a narrow country, lots of trees, rivers, lakes, and a sea of people. Th. picks me up at the airport; his face is ordinary, the face of a stranger. Th. is a writer. Since he opened his restaurant, the Tay Bac Flower, he has stopped writing. Before I came here, I thought I had read all of Th's stories. He had a way of writing each sentence as if he were hacking at the trunk of a banana tree with a machete, making the sap spurt out of it.

Th. takes us to a bookstore. Miss T. and I rush

around, poring over the books. Th's complete works have just been reprinted, including *Nha Nam Rain*. I have never read it. Miss T is beautiful, radiant, always laughing. She has come back to Nha Nam a hundred times and still isn't bored. We all go out for a drink. A street kid hassles us, wants to shine our shoes.

"Men study computer science, women prostitute themselves, kids shine shoes, hawk lottery tickets. Where's the future?" I ask.

"In computer science, prostitution, hawking lottery tickets," Th. replies, indifferent.

We go back to Th's house. The lychee orchard is in full bloom. The trees curve all the way up to the Bai Vong mountains, their white blossoms like rippling silk. Th. is pensive. Miss T. goes to take a shower. The phone rings. Miss T. answers, holding the portable receiver above the rush of the water.

Nha Nam is like Con Son, I say.

Nha Nam is Con Son, Th. replies.

Th's wife serves dinner: two pieces of fried fish marinated in lemon grass, mussel soup, and a raw lotus-shoot salad. His wife is like millions of other women. Th. points at our chopsticks, inviting us to start. We should wait for Miss T., I say. Th's wife takes the child into the kitchen. In the evenings the Nha Nam rain falls, a sheet of silk unfurling all the way to the foot of the mountains. In a few days, says Th., he will take us to the opera, to see Le Sat duel Lieu Thang. For Nha

Namese, the price is 20,000 *nhn* a ticket. For overseas Nha Namese and foreigners it is triple.

"I'm Nha Namese too. Why the difference?"

"Nha Nam has its inferiors and superiors, its first and second-class bunks; here we have civilized people, and illiterates and thieves." Th. puffs on his water pipe. The room is thick with the acrid smoke. Th. is part intellectual, part hick. Now he owns a restaurant, flirts with capitalism. All that's left is the faintest scent of Tay Bac flower, a whiff of the dream.

Pouring rain. Miss T. is still in the shower. Th. goes out to buy rice wine from Mount Ma Yen, where Lieu Thang was decapitated. Drinking it is like drinking fetid blood, hot, bitter. Th. comes back with the wine. He and I sit there, watching the Nha Nam rain erase the water buffalo tracks in the mud. There is no place like Nha Nam. Cars and water buffaloes come and go on the same street. Time in Nha Nam is long, lazy, time enough to count all the hooves and tires on the road.

Miss T. finishes her shower, still on the phone. The receiver in one hand, she combs her hair with the other. She loves making her appointments, frivolous, last-minute, aimless, but full of passion. I have known Miss T. for a long time. I still don't understand what she wants out of life. Th. watches Miss T, his eyes glazed, unseeing. She is from another world, no longer a Nha Nam woman. Th. understands. He also knows that the scent of the Tay Bac flower can only be smelled, never captured.

The atmosphere is heavy. Th. insists I empty my glass. He spreads the table on the verandah. Earth smells mix with the shampoo scent of Miss T's hair, the Mount Ma Yen rice wine. Rain shrouds the mountains, the lychee orchard, reaching Th's front yard. It is like sitting in front of a marsh. Miss T. throws a pebble into the water, shattering the bubbles. Th. pulls up chairs, leans against a pillar inscribed with Chinese characters.

"Once, Nguyen Ung Long taught here," says Th. He gestures to a rotten wooden bench in the corner. "Nguyen Trai wrote poetry where you are seated." He points at Miss T.

She laughs, radiant as ever.

"And the place where you're seated?" I ask. I take a piece of fish with my chopsticks, nibbling the bone.

"Help yourself," Th. says to Miss T, and begins to eat. "Which period? Before or after Ho Quy Ly?" he asks me.

"Before."

"The Venerable Old Dan."

"After?"

"Rascals!"

Miss T. howls with laughter. Th. and I don't laugh.

It's stifling. Still raining but hot. Th. polishes off the pot of rice in the blink of an eye. I have nothing more to say. I gaze at the walls covered with red and gold Chinese characters. Th. is saying how Nguyen Trai was a genius, how once this house was part of the Venerable Tran Nguyen Dan's great Bang Ho estate. Later it was divided into smaller houses.

Th's regional-specialties restaurant is profitable. He bought one of the estate houses and had it redone it to preserve the soul of the motherland. The famous poet Nguyen Trai, he tells us, used to compose poetry here in a trance, without brush or paper. All he had to do was glance at the wall; calligraphy just appeared.

"One hundred and fifty poems in the national script; Nguyen Trai looked a hundred times. History can never be erased," says Th.

"Poetry is wit," I say. "You don't need to work with your hands and feet."

Miss T. laughs.

Th. chants a poem: "*At the road's end, Nguyen is dead, why cry?*"

"That verse isn't on the wall anymore," notices Miss T.

"I thought history could never be erased," I say.

"It can't," grumbles Th. "But the previous owner rippled it off and sold it to Taiwan."

Evening falls. We get up to leave. Th. asks where we are going. Drinking, I say.

He clucks his tongue. "Here you drink, overseas you drink. No difference."

"Why should there be? I'm Nha Namese."

I drive Miss T. on the back of a Honda Cub motorcycle. The road is slippery. The motorcycle weaves, veering into the lychee orchard. A million branches splay out, like hands of young girls pawing us. I dodge them, nearly lose my balance. Trampled white lychee flowers scatter the ground. The motorcycle plunges into a ditch, rain water sloshing over the sides. We wade across, up to our knees.

Miss T. grabs my shoulder. "Did you see the girls at the edge of the road?" she shouts into my ear.

"Where?"

"Just then, running through the orchard."

"That's Nha Nam for you."

Miss T. giggles. I steer the motorcycle, imagining her face behind me, beautiful when she laughs, ordinary when she is sad. We had promised to return to Nha Nam together. Back overseas, I asked her whether she wasn't bored of Nha Nam after coming back so many times? Going out here was just like going out any-where, she said. In Nha Nam happiness and sadness were all mixed up.

Leaving the orchard, the Dreams motorcycle takes off, veering wildly. I avoid looking at the girls, almost fall off again.

"Careful!" cries Miss T.

"Hey, we're not going to die, are we? *Life is still so beautiful, love is still so beautiful,*" I croon.

"You devil!" snaps Miss T.

Th. races after, his Honda Cub 70 roaring. But we had already reached the center of town. Thi Sach Street, Le Quy Don Street, Nguyen Du Street, Ngo Quyen Street, Pham Ngu Lao Street. Buffalo Blues Restaurant,

Q Bar, Doors Pub, Apocalypse Now Bar, the Venus Club . . .

I pull the motorcycle into the Guns 'n' Roses Bar. The parking lot attendant hands us a receipt. Th. gives up the race, drives past. He knows that Nha Nam has its superiors and inferiors, its insiders and outsiders, and in certain bars it's 50,000 *nhn* a drink.

We are overseas Nha Namese.

Near dawn, news comes that the archbishop has died. They say that before dying he lost the power of speech. Many Christians are in mourning. Miss T. and I leave the restaurant. The flags on the church are at half mast. We cross the empty street. Shops are closed. Not for mourning, but because dew still glistens on the leaves of the flame tree. The church is draped in purple silk. Statues are tied with black cloth. The streets are cold, empty. Miss T. says we should go to Th.'s house. I say we should go to the opera, to see Le Sat duel Lieu Thang.

"All you like is violence," she says, critical. She doesn't laugh.

The motorcycle crosses the orchard; the flowers aren't open yet, a pale white. Th's house has a big earthenware pot planted with a weeping cherry. The heady perfume carries all the way to the mountains.

Th. stayed up all night waiting for us. His face is creased, patient. He sees us and revs the motorcycle. The two Hondas race, side by side. Miss T., in a skirt, rides side saddle, her white shoes dangling. The wind is cool, the trees silent, the dirt road a dark red. The Hondas pass the Tu Phuc pagoda.

"When King Ly Thai Ton banished Nguyen Trai from the imperial court, Trai was the caretaker here," says Th., pointing at the pagoda. He chants another poem:

"How many millennia after a hero's passing does resentment smolder?"

"A poem by Nguyen Trai?" Miss Th. asks.

Th. nods.

I'm puzzled. "Why can't we see that inscription on the wall anymore?"

"They banned it," replies Th.

The Hondas roar. The path up to the Chi Lang Gate is winding. We have to keep shifting gears. The landscape changes. The clouds turn gray, the mountains darken, the green of the kohlrabi fields deepens. Truck tire tracks crisscross the fields.

"Damned Chinese traders. They come through these fields a hundred times a day," explains Th.

"Where are the Le Sats to stop them?"

"Busy building hotels," says Th. He revs his motorcycle, lurching forward. We rush down the steep hill like running water, the motorcycle brakes squealing louder than pigs at slaughter. We pay to get into the theater parking lot: 20,000 per ticket for Nha Namese, 60,000 for overseas Nha Namese.

"The woods were teeming with the righteous Lam Son rebel troops. Spears and swords flew, as if the entire region had sprouted spikes. The wind howled. The victory flag rippled and writhed like a snake. Le Thi was clad in armor. His body stocky, his brow low. Luu Nhan Chu and Le Linh were stark naked, their bodies tattooed. Le Sat swirled his glistening cutlass. Nguyen Trai stopped his steed in front of Oath Canyon. In his silk robes, he was as pretty as a maiden. The gong clanged six times; the Chinese Ming troops charged down from the Devil's Gate. Le Sat put his horse to the trot through the Ham Quy and Cat Linh mountain passage. Their veins and muscles taut, pulsing, men and horses rode through the ramparts. The conquering Chinese duke, Lieu Thang, lifted his club to strike. Le Sat turned his horse, retrieving his spear in a gesture of pure, flaming beauty. Children fought over the decapitated head. A gang of them kicked it around. Le Sat took his dagger and stabbed Lieu Thang's side, extracted his liver. He placed it in a jar filled with medicinal wine."

Miss T. closes her eyes.

On the way back that afternoon, the road is dusty, the sun lazes.

Miss T. and I are puzzled. "Just then, on stage, was that a real death?" she asks.

"All deaths are real, none are fake," Th. grumbles.

Miss T. is still terrified. I drive, she clutches my waist, her hands clammy. The scent of the weeping cherry from the Bai Vong mountain doesn't cover the stench of blood. Th's wife has already served lunch: chopped snake meat, snake blood pudding, crispy fried snake skin, snake and rice porridge with lotus seeds. Miss T. doesn't touch her chopsticks.

That evening, news comes that VC, the famous musician has died. Miss T. is sad. We go out to the café at the corner of Nguyen Du Street. Madame Dai's restaurant is doing a booming business since the French president's visit and all the photos. At the end of the street, the Buffalo Blues Restaurant plays jazz. Besides eating and drinking, there's nothing to do in Nha Nam, says Miss T. We sit there, listening to the music. The year before, when I came back, I felt like I was revisiting the past; this year it's like stepping into the future. The past was cruel, the future is cruel.

Miss T. talks about the musician's death. She asks if we're going to the funeral. I shake my head. Each generation dies its own death. Evening falls, the fading sunlight blooms on the skin of the shoe-shine boys. "Rainwater skin," like in Marguerite Duras' novel *The Lover*. We ask the waiter to play S. music, the singer Hz, the hit song "The Call of Sunlight." Miss T. and I listen to it over and over. In Nha Nam, where we live beneath the sun. The lyrics move us. The singer calls the sun so passionately. Sunlight dies on the rivers, on the roads. The word "death" repeated over and over.

Miss T. goes back to N's place. I drop her off at February Second Street.

Late at night, at Th's house, a purple mist shrouds the lychee orchard. Venerable Tran Nguyen Dan's estate is quiet, motionless. The clay pot that holds the weeping cherry tree is icy to the touch. Th. disappears down the dark path. An oil lamp flickers weakly. Rotten bamboo blinds face the rear courtyard and the mountains beyond.

I call to Th. My cry echoes across the mountains. The silhouette of a maiden flits through the garden, her silk robes dissolving like moonlight. I fell in love with Nguyen Trai on the eve of the full moon, the fourteenth day of the lunar calendar. On that day the night's face is perfect, bathed with moonlight.

Nguyen Trai's back is slim; the poems appear as if painted in the air. Nighttime in the lychee orchard, his footsteps are music, smiling like a bud of spring flower.

"More poetry!" I shout after him.

"At the southern edge of the capital."

Nguyen Trai smiles, sad. "At the southern edge of the capital, a one-room hut. I've drunk my fill of water, I hunger for food."

The moon fades. The night grows pale. The poem is left unfinished.

When I drive downtown, I find Miss T, her shoulders drenched in sunlight. According to the calendar on the wall, it's the twelfth. The musician VC died on the tenth. I had stayed in the lychee orchard for two whole days. During that time Miss T. went to Da Nang, swam in the sea at Non Nuoc beach. Her skin is tanned, salt-scrubbed. Two days in the lychee orchard and I had missed the news: the imperialists had renewed diplomatic relations with Nha Nam! Miss T. takes me to see people chugging beer. It is like a cascade. All of Nha Nam is celebrating. At noon, we rent a van, a Renault Espace, to go to Nghe An. The bus is fast, runs smoothly. Th. drives, lecturing us the whole way:

"In the year of the Snake, King Le Loi stormed the city of Nghe An, captured Ly An and Phuong Chinh. The righteous Lam Son rebel troops pitched their tents along the Lam River. One night, in the Pho Ho Temple of Trao Khau village, the king had a nightmare. His body was chilled, his lips cracked, he had a vision of waves crashing, wind howling, flagpoles falling, ships sinking. He awoke the next morning drenched in sweat, his feet numb, his face ashen. His counselor, Nguyen Trai, spoke respectfully: 'It is an omen, my lord. The Water God is calling for your wife. But his majesty must avenge the Lam Son, restore justice, replace bandits with men of virtue, violence with a great cause. You should not be superstitious.' But the nightmare obsessed the king, who feared for his life. 'Once, King Ly, stricken with an eye disease, had been cured thanks to the sacrifice of a couple who jumped into the Thien Phu River, offering their bodies to the Water God.' the king reflected. 'Do you call that superstition?' Nguyen Trai said nothing. The curtains stank."

I pull the van into the parking lot overlooking the river. The surface of the river teems with boats filled with tourists. Miss T. and I buy first-class tickets, right below the stage.

The king stands on a pedestal, his back is three feet wide, his eyes determined. Nguyen Trai is nearby, holding the royal coffer. Tran Nguyen Han holds the royal parasol. Le Le and Le Ngan stand guard with clubs; the royal troops march past the stand, their blood red flags flapping. The rumble of gongs and drums fills the air. The north wind blows the clouds, bells ring. The king points at the Lam River, shouting: "Today, for the sake of my people, I offer my wife as a sacrifice to the Water God. I vow to storm Dong Quan, to make Ngoc Tran's son crown prince." A thunder of firecrackers. Le Sat stabs a horse and collects the blood. Soldiers drag the queen, Ngoc Tran, from the stand. Young, beautiful, her eyes are like willow leaves, her lips as red as berries. She holds her bawling three-year-old son, Nguyen Long. Le Sat lowers his cudgel. The soldiers lock her in a cage. Nguyen Long howls for his mother. The cage sinks to the bottom of the Lam River, Ngoc Tran writhing. Waves crash. A handful of her hair floats to the surface.

Miss T's face is ashen.

On the way back, Miss T. and I are anxious, unnerved. Before stopping, Th. asks "Care for any more games?"

"That's enough," Miss T. replies.

I avoid looking at Th. The vision of the hair still floating on the water. On the thirteenth day, the Month of the Monkey, Year of the Pig, I return to Old Dan's house. My fingers stiff with anger, I drive, Miss T. behind me. A logging truck runs into us. The workers flee. Miss T's head is injured, a brain hemorrhage no one diagnoses when we carry her to the emergency room at the No. 1 District Hospital in Nguyen Tri Phuong. She is delirious, can't speak. The doctor on duty criticizes her for being "uncooperative." I argue with them, finally rent an ambulance to Cho Ray, the biggest hospital in Nha Nam. It is poor, dirty, people camped out in the halls and staircases, waiting for treatment. Miss Nh., a friend of Miss T's, hears the news and comes to visit, pays the hospital fees. The doctor diagnoses a brain hemorrhage that requires surgery. Miss T. is unconscious. Miss Nh's family goes off to buy blood for the transfusions, sterile needles, antibiotics. I go to look for Th.

"This is surreal!" I scream.

Th. sits reading, his eyes bloodshot.

"Nobody can invent the truth," he snaps.

But he just stands there, watching me as I smash Old Dan's temple. The lychee orchard lies in ruins, the mountains hang low, the clouds wispy. I go back to the hospital. Miss T. is still unconscious, on a respirator. The incision is bruised. Her hospital bed is rusty. I wait outside her room in the corridor. Relatives care for their sick, sleeping on the stairs, lying everywhere, all the way out to the hospital garden. Nha Nam mothers weep silently. The hospital looks like a leper colony.

I leave Nha Nam at the end of the month of the Monkey. Miss T. is still in the hospital, her right hand and leg still paralyzed. Th. sees me off at the airport, his face like a million others, still unfamiliar.

The plane reaches cruising height. I read Th's story "Nha Nam Rain," the passage where Di Than rides his horse through the tropical rain, weeping over life, for having sold a woman to a cruel fate. Th. begins the story with contempt for everything:

> I'm telling this story, young man, shut up, you're too young, you're an idiot. I'm telling this story, young lady, because you're going to get married and then it'll be only trouble. No one will ever tell you stories.

He ends with a sentence devoid of emotion: *This story ends here.*

I close the book. The plane flies smoothly. We're at thirty thousand feet. From this height the Nha Nam rain is crystal clear, a jewel.

THE DRAGON HUNT

We're still very young. You can't tell from our faces, our eyes, but from our insatiable dreams. The Year of the Dog. I come back to live on Quy's estate, in the south of the continent. The earth turns, a block of knotty stone, chipping off the invisible tips of its jagged spines. Every afternoon Quy, Chien, another guest, and I raise our glasses, inviting to our feast the invisible beings that all three of us clearly sense are present. Riding the waves of the trees of the forest, they glide right up to our verandah, scamper down the mountainside to our table. Quy's estate is vast, imposing.

Quy pours anisette liqueur into three glasses. The alcohol gleams. The shadow of the fifty clan houses that crowd around us is reflected in the bottoms of the glasses, abrupt, threatening. Every time I contemplate Quy's estate, I get goose pimples, shiver with fear. In fact, this is no ordinary residence, but a kind of grandiose funeral temple that proudly dominates the entire mountain range. Fifty houses built in the ancient style, whose columns pierce the clouds. Nine enormous bronze urns stand in the front courtyard. In the rear courtyard Quy has built an artificial lake patterned after the Three Seas Lake in Mau Ninh. An intimidating landscape. No mere mortal residence.

Quy's wife, Phuong, serves us a platter of hors d'oeuvres: fine slivers of heart, barely poached, thin coils of intestine, firm and white, like a woman's nipples. Phuong is beautiful; she has the bewitching beauty of Northern women, a smirk that scampers along the rims of her slender eyelids before darting toward two spiky green chilies in the bowl of dipping sauce.

Quy reaches out and spears a spindly piece of intestine, bites into the chewy flesh, elastic as the nipple of a breast. He tells us how once it was a horrible thing to eat dragon meat. Dismembering the beast was a solemn rite; strapping young men would tie it up, then wait for the first village elder to read a funeral oration before slitting its throat. Now, here in this country, you can find deep-frozen dragon meat in precooked packets; all you have to do is buy it, let it thaw, then eat your fill. Quy roars with laughter. The chopsticks dance between his fingers, then dart toward the plate of bloodred phoenix hearts. I shudder.

"Eating heart reminds you of your friends!" Quy chuckles.

When we first met, a long time ago, I noticed his gaunt face, pale lips, and sunken cheeks, the traces of the malaria he had contracted back when he served in the resistance on Front B, and which still ravages him from time to time. Since he bought his fifty houses, Quy's complexion has totally changed. The only memorial left to those exhausting ten years fighting along the Truong Son mountain range is a gracious row of white sandalwood trees along the wall bordering the property. Quy commemorates his youth in Hanoi in the pure milky white flowers of a grove of alstonia trees.

As Quy watches me contemplate the garden, he guesses my thoughts. "The trees are from Hanoi. I ordered them back there. That alstonia tree used to stand on Hang Gai Street, remember?"

"You were able to buy it?"

I start at the sound of a butcher's knife. Quy's wife, her back hunched over, has just hacked a kidney in two. Her fingers stroke, then squeeze the gleaming, sticky balls on the cutting board. She caresses them tenderly, turning them over and over, rhythmically lifting out the fetid nerves, then cutting shallow furrows with slices of the blade. Phuong scoops some water from the Three Seas Lake to rinse off the kidneys. She sprinkles them with some dried basil, then wraps them in strips of lard before skewering them.

After the skewers are finished, Phuong goes off to look for charcoal in the house. Quy pays no attention to his wife. He grabs a sprig of basil, clucking his tongue. "Everything goes today. We're selling everything."

Quy pours more anisette, tips his chin toward the sky. The alcohol, like a green snake, runs down his throat, slips under his Adam's apple, and wriggles before disappearing into his gut. I empty the fragrant glass that Quy offers me. Pure anise, thick, penetrating. Diluted in a bit of water, it gives off an aphrodisiac scent and shimmers in gilded reflection that, like smoke, invades the senses, intoxicating. The alcohol thins my blood, makes my muscles and nerves tingle. I feel an anise flower unfurl and bloom in the soles of my feet.

Chien remains silent. He's not laconic, but he wears the stamp of our era, the seal of death, the indelible proof of a reality erased, discarded by history. Every time I sit next to him, I notice how his whole body gives off that strange aura, how the face of destiny is etched into the slit of his eyes, the ridge of his nose, his jaw, his faded hair, his flabby muscles. What's frightening, even though he's here, facing me, is that I don't see him at all. As if he were totally erased. He no longer exists in the history books. Only the past, from time to time, erupts from his body to bump against Quy.

"So your *bo doi* commandoes liked to drink this stuff?" Chien snickers.

"Who told you that?" Quy snaps back, hacking up a dragon. He scrapes off the scales, grabs a chunk of raw kidney on the edge of the cutting board, and pops it in his mouth.

"When I was in the resistance, this piece stank; we saved it to use as medicine, for stomach cramps. A banquet like the one we're having today was beyond our wildest dreams. Even today you can't find any back there. Up north, in Cao Bang and Lao Cai, there are fewer trees than in Hanoi."

"So it's come to that?" I sigh, emptying another glass of Pastis, swimming with ice cubes. This brew is strange; the more you drink, the more you have to have it. No wonder so many of the natives here go mad drinking it. After the fourth glass my head spins. A rain of golden flowers. Petals dance in the wind, burrow through my skin, my flesh, sprouting young anise roots that writhe and squirm in me. Vegetation spreads, thickens; undergrowth surrounds me, besieges me. How strange, how voluptuous, this feeling of melting into nature, of dissolving into the grass, into earth and stone, how it explodes inside me. I sense the presence of invisible beings standing in the courtyard. Right under my eyes, the mountainside plunges over a bottomless precipice. I reach out, grab the bottle of alcohol. Here, in this essence of anise, nature is also present. Sun streams like lava down my throat.

Quy doesn't look at anyone. He picks at a piece of poached brain with his chopsticks, dips it in salt and pepper, bites into a sprig of parsley, and swallows the whole thing.

"A few years ago, the Chinese came to Vietnam to buy the anise roots, willing to pay a high price. Villagers throughout the province started to dig up all the plants and sell them off. Crafty bastards."

"They may be crafty, but we're naïve," Chien quips, contemptuous, swallowing half a phoenix heart. Quy glowers at him but lets the remark pass. He pushes the slices of meat into a dish and scrapes the cutting board. He has the swift, neat, practiced gestures of the Chinese street vendors who hawk intestines marinated in soy sauce. Chien doesn't say another word. For several months now, aside from a few moments of tension, Chien has accepted that Quy rides the high tide of history. His silence is half humiliation, half defeat. To forget, he tries to drown Quy and I in alcohol. Adding a bit of water to the anisette, a few ice cubes, he drinks, repeating this three or four times without pausing. The bottle of Pastis has barely been opened, and the plate of intestines is already finished.

Quy laboriously chews a tough piece of intestines; he grimaces. "These old dragons are just as tough as water buffalo."

Quy fishes out a red chili, sucks its pointy end, tasting it at the tip of his tongue. I'm waiting for his daughter, Nu, to appear. She's just come back from her lycée; I watch her cross the gate to the estate. The architecture of Quy's estate is like an imperial tomb with its well-aligned columns in the front courtyard, the sacred tortoises with stone stelae perched on their backs. Once, Quy explained to me: "So that our children, according to the ancient traditions of our people, will be able to carve their names here when they get into the best universities." Nu passes our table without greeting us. Quy scolds her. "You brat! Didn't anybody ever teach you any manners? Don't you even say hello?"

"*Je n'ai pas faim,*" Nu replies, slamming the door to her room. Quy sighs, pulls a wooden case out from under the table. A dozen bottles of red wine. Furrowing his brow, he opens a bottle: "The girls here have no breeding anymore."

"Time to play cards!" Chien announces. Two hands marked by the war throw a wad of bills on the table. Quy shuffles a deck, hands it to me to cut, then distributes the cards with the same agile, expert motion he used to chop the meat. I take my hand, gazing at Quy's wife, who has just entered the garden. She sets a grill on the barbecue, and fans the flames. Smoke billows, masking the trunk of a flamboyant tree. Seeing the cards, she cries out: "Wait for me! I want to play too!"

"There's no place for women in this game," Quy grumbles, still fuming at his daughter. But Phuong is not the submissive type. Her face hardens. "Women are people too!" Quy gives in, deals the cards again into four piles. The heat this afternoon is stifling. The embers under the grill, which is spread with kidneys, redden and glow with each flick of Phuong's fan. She quickly turns the chunks of kidney, then pulls them off. The kidneys are still rare, but shrunken and firmed by the flames.

Chien empties a few glasses of wine and announces the rules: no bankruptcy. He fixes the value of the combinations: five hundred francs for each combination. A suit of dragons from one to thirteen is worth thirteen points, thirteen points for the square as well as for a suit of five cards of the same color. But the dragon suit takes all. I look at my cards: a blood-colored set. A single color; I know I'm going to win and we haven't even started playing. Next to me, Phuong snaps her hand. She spreads the cards open and closes them, then opens them again. After each move she glances furtively around, her scarlet lips pursing, then opening slightly in a faint smile. I'm falling into a trance from the alcohol; Phuong looks beautiful, sharp, ferocious. She's wearing a see-through blouse. Beads of sweat run down her breasts. I want her, feel like having her, right there.

"Are you ready? What, are you going to take the whole day for just thirteen cards? Open your eyes! Take a look!"

Impatient, Quy slaps his hand down, right in front of Chien, who has just shown his own. Caustic, Chien says: "Three pairs and a suit. Take that, if you can!"

"Three of a kind!"

Phuong suddenly shows her hand. But the one I'm holding trumps them all. We play another six games; I win five. Every two games Phuong uncorks another bottle of red wine. Pommerol, Chateau Rouget, 1985.

Quy lifts his glass in a toast: "To our ten years of anti-American resistance!"

Chien corrects him: "To our ten years' struggle against communism!"

"What bullshit," Phuong snickers.

After the ninth bottle, I'm seeing stars. Cards dance before my eyes. The ripe, raw red of the wine blazes like Phuong's lips, like her tongue, melting in my mouth like the thigh of a very young woman, evaporates, flooding my head like a noisy flock of crows that peck at my temples. My body feels weightless, I lose control of my hands and feet; they detach from my body, floating here and there. "I'm gonna faint," I say to Quy.

"Deserter!" snaps Chien. Quy jumps up, opens my eyelids, examines my eyes. "It's all over. He's dying. Boil water. Make him a Turkish tea! Hurry!"

My stomach swells. All the food, lungs, dragon meat,

kidneys, brain, unicorn meat, liver, heart, and gizzards, churn in my stomach, rising in my throat. Through a cloud of stars I can see fleeting shadows, Chien and Phuong, running, clutching me by the arm, cradling me by the nape of the neck. I see Quy run into the house and return with a metal box. My veins explode. I feel nauseous, but Chien restrains me, his huge hand pressing against my throat to stop me from vomiting. I thrash about, struggle with him. Empty bottles in front of me shatter into crystal shards. Chien steps on one, his blood gushes. Reflected in the glass I see my shriveled face awash in Chien's purple blood. Chien, oblivious, continues to thump my chest, massaging my heart with his hands. Each press of his hand makes my body jump. Phuong's face looms over mine, coming down over me like an enormous basket. I writhe and thrash.

"Come on, drink up!" Phuong shouts. She slaps my cheeks, pours more tea. Scalding hot liquid singes my tongue, numbing it. It's strong, bitter. I feel my body melt and liquefy as it goes down. The scorching late afternoon sun hits me full in the face. Monstrous, this estate. In my drunkenness I see a dragon's tail surface and undulate above Quy's lands, his fifty houses. I see it plunge its two trunks into Three Seas Lake, sucking up water. Is this rain, a storm, a tempest, thunder and lightning, or just a dragon spouting water? I don't know anymore, dazzled by the incandescent glitter of the dragon's scales. Chien heaves me onto his shoulder and carries me to my room. From the garden I hear Quy's shouts echoing, praising the beauty of the beast.

We're still very young. You can't tell from our faces, our eyes, but from our insatiable dreams. For four thousand years in my native land death was natural, the result of the body's decay. But my generation, oddly enough, seeks it out, while our bodies are still intact.

We stare out at the sea from the dunes. I shiver. I'm going to die, I think. A savage, violent death. The sky unfurls toward the distant west, bluer and bluer, limitless, illuminating the ocean. All of us have our eyes riveted on the unimaginable blue: the Pacific sky, the sky of the west, over there, where we are going to die. My guts starts to wrench from fear mixed with a strange, frenzied desire. Amidst the howl of sirens, three boats moor on the quays. Low barges shrouded in black sheets embroidered with glass beads that form elaborate wreaths of fake flowers, a kind of funeral vessel that I will lie down in, next to twelve hundred other human beings. Three barges carry the corpses. My body is clammy, icy with terror. Mother stands at my side. I can hear her breathing, halting, rhythmic, heavy with love. She accompanies me to the threshold of my voyage to the other world. I am afraid, but I don't beg her to keep me back with her. Yearning, the dream of a new life, merge inside me, compel me to leave. I yearn for both life and death. Strange, my own mother doesn't try to hold me back, but I can read the pain on her face. The pain of childbirth, when flesh splits and skin cracks, when the uterus tears, the placenta bursts. When the blood flows. Pain, pain that we know is coming, and yet which never overcomes the desire to give life.

I inherited my masochism from my mother; I prepare myself for the first painful joys of my life. Ahead of me in line, my friends commit suicide, one by one. They embalm the corpses in the belly of the boat. I watch as the mothers' bodies bend and fall, despairing. I watch their eyes roll upward, their faces stiffen in rigor mortis. Young eyes that still strain, even at the final moment of parting, to frame images of their country, their families. Now it's my turn. Mother wails, moans, her body writhing in agony, but she doesn't try to shield me, doesn't spread her arms open to hug me to her bosom, the sacred gesture of mothers everywhere to protect their children. After four thousand years the mothers of my country have changed; they're ready to witness our death, ready to barter their children's lives in exchange for their dreams. They organize our mass suicide. And Mother and I, we are accomplices. I climb down into the boat, my feet trembling; I don't even have time to turn and take one last look at my mother when a sailor jumps on me, sinking an ax into my skull. The blade splits my brain, erasing part of my memory. My blood spurts, flowing onto the deck, red as the flesh of a *gac* fruit, glistening, innocent, in the sunlight. I collapse, swimming in a pool of my own blood. Mother's blood. I'm not dead yet, but the blood rises over my face. I cry for her. The skipper rushes over to help the sailor, brandishing shears used to cut barbed wire; he cuts out my tongue, forbids me to call to my mother in our mother tongue. I struggle. The boat owner barks orders to the pilot to raise anchor, hammers nails into my eyes, blinding me; I can't see the motherland anymore. I scream as they shred my flesh, scatter it. But my tongue is gone, cut off. I can only let out moans, choked, soundless, silent gasps that echo for me alone. No one reacts, intervenes. No one takes pity on us. Total indifference. The boat leaves the quays.

It's not that my people have lost all feeling. But they've seen too much. Too much death. Dreams are their only hope, the only thing left of lasting value. To them we are lucky corpses.

Sailors dismember corpses with a saw, selling them off, chunk by chunk to the pirates. Electric saws shriek and howl like carnivorous beasts. They throw our bloody entrails overboard. Our guts float, the current carrying them back to the motherland. They toss our bones overboard too; they sink, deep down, to the bottom, into the bowels of the sea. Waves crest, a storm gathers, rocks and coral reefs loom just beneath the surface. Deep, dark, unfathomable mouths lie in wait for us. Our limbs fall, helpless, unable to hold onto the boat; they flap in the wind, then sink. But when the sailor splits open my skull, I try to bolt. Who can accept to die trampled and crushed underfoot, let alone sawed apart? I squirm and thrash, twisting my head from side to side to dodge the blade. Steel saws screech and grind near my temples, I cry, sob, pray, beg them to spare me. It's like a furnace in this cabin. Rubber mats, stacked one on top of another on the deck, pitch and sway, rising and falling, swooning in the stifling tropical heat. The ceiling spins like a top, picks up speed, grazing my body. Sweat beads in my armpits, down my back, my clammy thighs. My mattress is soaked with salty water, gluey with algae. Sea water floods into the room. I swim in an ocean of sweat, swim for my life, thrashing, groping for a way out; I pound the bed with my feet, my fists, scream for mother. I toss, feverish, in the sheets. I throw off the covers, claw my pillow. I pull the mosquito netting off the window, fling it open, let the sun wash over me, like falls, cascading and bursting over me, expelling me from my nightmare.

I am panting. My body glistens with thousands of tiny beads of sweat released by the suffocating air of this room. But it still clings to me, my nightmare, to my clammy, livid body; the pumping of Chien's hands on my chest echoes the blows of the sailors' hammers. Jagged hiccups rattle in my throat. Fear, death, resurrection; and now this intermittent lucidity, like the calm between two seizures. Blood trickles from my nose, drips into my mouth.

It takes me a long time to come to my senses, to leave those barbaric days, to return to this reality. Silence, everywhere. I am here now, I realize, stretched out in the middle of my room at Quy's. A ceiling fan whirs listlessly, creaking, incapable of stirring the slightest breeze. I don't know when Quy installed it; this morning it wasn't there. The fan watches me, inquisitorial. I stretch out a hand, touch the wet, moss-covered walls. The room Quy gave me is built against the side of a mountain; all you have to do is open the door to touch huge, wild boulders. I can hear the water trickling at the bottom of Three Seas Lake. Usually, it flows silently in the murky depths, but today it roars, bellows. The afternoon yawns wider, spreads. I don't know how long I've been lying in this room; I hear every noise, distinctly. Grass struggling to grow around the house. Wooden pillars creaking on the verandah. Moths crawling in the crevices of the wood. Eggshells cracking in the chicken roost. And amidst these breaking sounds the fragile stirring of seedlings, sprouting, craning their necks under my bed. My room is covered with them. A pool of my vomit spreads, sticky, reeking, on the carpet. I hear my blood race, the veins pulsing in my chest, my muscles, my brain, my penis. I hear the rumble of cells in my body as they are born and then die, tumultuous, seething, wave after wave, in an endless cycle, an infinite harmony of creation and destruction, life and death, and these sounds, insistent, relentless, sweep away my nightmare.

It's raining; I don't know when it began. The eerie light of dusk flickers out, vanishes behind a murky veil of fog that shrouds the house. It's pouring now. Huge, leaden raindrops thud and echo like the sound of the shovels that the natives plunge, every morning, into the ground surrounding Quy's estate. Generous, the rain pours over the balcony, floods into my room, showering the potted kumquat plants. A cool, gently shivering mist steals through my window, rustling through the moss on the walls. The craggy boulders at the edge of my room spring to life again, their bodies stirring, bathed by the rain. This unexpected rain cleanses me of the last, haunting traces of the dream. I return to myself, oddly lucid, my spirit bathed in a sudden serenity, as if the rain had diluted the effect of the Turkish tea. I lie there, contemplating the rain as it spreads, evenly, over Quy's lands, a blanket of molten silver. Desire for a woman overwhelms me.

Suddenly Phuong appears on my doorstep.

"You hid here to wait for me, didn't you?" she coos, giggling intimately. She bends down at the foot of my bed, stretches her body toward me, and bites my ear, murmuring: "Waited for me long enough? Old Quy really kept an eye on me. It took me ages to find an excuse to come inside and talk to Nu. Did you miss me?" Phuong whispers as she slips her hand under my shirt, caresses my chest. Her soft, cool hands open like anise flower petals, graze my skin, fragrant, exciting. Phuong strokes and smooths my hair, wipes away the last of my tears. Her gestures are tender, soft. She is no longer hard-edged, brazen, as she was earlier in the garden. But I can't decide; after all, she is Quy's wife. I try to wriggle from her hands. She bursts out laughing. "So, you're a shy one, are you?"

Phuong presses her body forward, takes my hand, rubs it against her breast, forces me to knead and fondle it. "Like that?" she coos again. "I liked you right away, when the old man introduced us. Do you want to sleep with me? Why didn't you tell on me earlier when I cheated at cards?"

"Why would I do that?"

Phuong bursts out laughing. "God, you're naïve. Now I know why Quy calls you a young innocent. But I like you. That's enough for me."

Phuong takes off her blouse, throws it into a corner of the room. Her big, firm ivory breasts are erect, determined. She suddenly glances at the pool of vomit on the carpet.

"So, you really were drunk?"

Without waiting for explanations, she bends over and licks the vomit. Hungrily, passionately, she swallows everything. Her quick, darting tongue laps up the lumps of meat. The pool shrinks, then disappears. Phuong sucks her fingers with regret. I was already aroused when Phuong stepped into the room, as soon as I heard her simpering voice. But the sight of a beautiful woman on her knees licking up my vomit only heightens my desire. Never had I seen anything more erotic than this: Phuong drinking the putrid, bitter liquid that my stomach had spread on the ground. My penis stiffens. I want to jump on Phuong, to grab her in my arms. She sees it and pounces, nibbling and biting at me.

"Just like an animal, wasn't I? Eating your puke."

Phuong swings her breasts, gives me a long, wild kiss. She wraps her arms around me, squeezes me tight, locking her fingers around me like tentacles. She unfastens my belt. The sheets are drenched in sweat; we embrace in the water, bobbing, diving, plunging into a pool of flesh. I feel faint with desire for her, feel like pushing her over, like pressing her head to the ground, laying her on her back, spreading her legs, raping her, quickly, at the foot of the bed, but my arms and legs are limp, leaden after my nightmare; they refuse to cooperate. Phuong looks me over, impatient. Her fingers feverishly fumble with my fly.

"You're still drunk. Let me help."

Her ripe red lips plunge and withdraw, rough, passionate. Phuong sucks vigorously, zealously, with the endurance of a woman used to tilling rice paddies; her lips are taut, greedy, possessive, engulfing. My whole body is suddenly covered with ants; they crawl over me, injecting their honeyed spears into my flesh. I feel my body slip from me, soar above the fields, gliding, riding the wind, then swooning as strange, primitive clouds, the spires of forests and mountains, pass through me. I hear my voice howl in the immense, infinite void; I drift on a current of clouds toward the sun, there where the rain has ceased to fall, the eye of the storm, where the sun has flickered out, but where it is still light, the shimmering, pulsing light of my youth.

The sea unfurls beneath me, a deep, terrifying blue. Suddenly, I recognize the beaches of my nightmare. I scream for Mother, grab Phuong's head, beg her to stop, but she keeps sucking, clutching me between her taut, passionate lips, swallowing hard as my body falls back into the sea of my doomed, suicidal childhood. I relive the panic, the terror, the odd thrill of chasing death, of willingly offering up my own body for torture. I float back, staggering across the ocean. Wind howls in my ears. My flesh grows younger, blossoming, my eyes clear, youth surges back into my body, I am full of life, vigor. I see the wharf again, the dunes of black sand, the sea teeming with rafts that carry people toward the boats. I see myself, a boy walking through a market. Phuong refuses to let go, continues frantically sucking me, swallowing me. My body arches and swells, like a kite drunk on the wind, billowing and flapping, soaring over rooftops, pagodas, temples, and markets. I see everything again. I want to step back on land, run home, fall into my mother's arms, but Phuong won't let me, grips me, her fingers still squeezing, wringing me. As if she were flying a kite, she forces me to rise higher in the air, higher and higher, until the explosion, until I fall onto the boat to be massacred. A machete splits my head, my shoulders, saws at my brain, my flesh, shattering my bones, my skull.

My blood trickles, slimy. I'm afraid. I shriek, howl, scream myself hoarse. A cry resonates through the room, echoing off the walls; the cry of a gut ripped apart, of childhood's end, a cry from my body, all the pent-up vitality imprisoned there, surges forth in my first ejaculation, overflowing in a strong, thick, ardent tide that washes over Phuong's face.

My breathing comes fast and halting, my body quakes and shudders, my veins go slack, snap, my penis hangs limp, a decapitated snake.

Phuong grabs the sheet and wipes the semen, still wriggling, from her hair, face, and lips. "I'll be back tonight." Her voice is tender, mischievous. She throws her shirt over her head and disappears. I shut my eyes.

I hear old Quy calling to her, his voice echoing from some deserted place, resounding farther and farther away, from another existence, another world, drifting through my room only to lose itself, to disappear somewhere else, far, far away.

Tet. The Year of the Dog. We're still very young. You can't tell from our faces, our eyes, or our skin, but from the dreams, engraved in us, that never leave us. Tet. The Year of the Dog. Every day is Tet; every year is the Year of the Dog. Every night ends in a New Year's Eve party; every day opens onto the new year. Time doesn't exist. Space doesn't exist. Concepts don't exist. There is no norm by which we can measure our lives. No one knows when, or how long it's been since I came back to live on Quy's estate. Even I don't know. All I know is that with each passing day his estate becomes more and more familiar to me. We have lived thousands of years under these roofs shaped like crab shells, among these columns, these colonnades, behind these antique panels, inside these walls. The forest behind the estate thickens with each day, the mountains advancing toward the continental shelf, plunging their feet in the sea, rooting themselves in the abyss; the sun rises in the north, the moon sets in the south, the earth is made up of ten continents, men live for a thousand years; we don't care. Quy continues to throw drinking parties; Chien continues to lose himself in the mystery of cards; I continue to come onto Phuong's radiant face.

Strange. Time doesn't exist, and yet I live in a state of innocence, purity. As if, suddenly, in a blinding flash, my childhood had come back. I am a child. Fifteen, maybe sixteen. Adolescence, an age swollen with desire, brimming with it. Innocent, restless, searching. So innocent I don't even blush when I see Phuong, as if I'd never slept with her. As if nothing had ever happened between us.

One morning, almost by instinct, I wander out of my room, mount the narrow spiral staircase of the Bao Nghiem Tower behind the Buddhist pagoda at the back of Quy's estate. The damp, moldy stairs, steeped in the vapors of the nocturnal storm, drip and ooze down onto the deserted corridors and galleries. I stumble into Dinh's painting studio, a labyrinth of rooms. I walk past wall after wall cluttered with paintings. Before Tet they all looked the same; now Dinh's paintings change every day. Hundreds of them, all pure white. From one room to the next, always the same style: fluttering white strokes that glide across the jute canvases. The icy, desolate whiteness of jade. Gazing at Dinh's paintings, I face the universe, its silence, its immensity. No dust. No mountains. No clouds. No people. Only an infinite, sinister, empty space. The white doesn't just cover the canvases; it bleaches the entire room. The walls, the carpet, the tables, the chairs, the ceiling, the floor. Dinh whitens everything with his brush. Only the teapot makes a noise that isn't white; the water boils feebly, tea leaves shiver and open like young buds. Dinh is seated, his back turned to me; he picks up a palette knife to spread the paint. The canvas shimmers, a quivering white, as if it had sucked up all the other colors mixed on his palette. Dinh squeezes his tubes of oils and colors, spreads the paint in thick patches and layers. Entire palettes of blue, gray, red, violet, black, yellow, disappear in a flash. Only the white is left. Only white paint is left encrusted on the palette knife. Dinh plunges his hands into the canvas, his whole body twisting and thrashing, wrestling with the painting. He grabs his knife with both hands and plunges it up to the handle into the painting. As if to kill, as if to finish someone off with a dagger. Dinh's body suddenly recoils, parrying a blow from some invisible force. Paint oozes and drips down the handle of his knife, colors congealing on his hand, sticky, like ropes tugging him, dragging him toward the canvas. His taut, hardened face goes slack, his gaze fading into the desperate look of a man swimming against the current, crossing the ocean in search of life. A tortured, miserable face, the face of a man who has used up all strength. Dinh's pupils glisten with the reflection of thousands of paintings, all terrifying, strange, monstrous. But the canvas is still white. The nerves in Dinh's wrists tighten, his wrists swell as if seized by tetanus, his sweat falling in drops on the ground. I sense that he is appealing to me for help. I grab him by the shoulders, shake him, try to wake him up, but I've barely touched him when my body is dragged, pushed, thrown onto the canvas. I collapse, my face splattered, my skin pierced, ripped by shards and splinters of decayed paint. Bleeding, I slip and slide, skating across layers of slick, sticky paint. I fall headlong into the gaping canvas, drowning under a thick rush of paint. But between two brush strokes I can see a long, narrow verandah, nooks and crannies, long corridors that open onto rooms cluttered with bizarre, extraordinary objects: a table with five legs; a diamond-shaped lightbulb; a cactus flower petal; a woman with a hexagonal face; a child with no eyes or mouth, a face as pale and thin as a yeast wafer; herds of strange beasts, water buffaloes with horses' heads; dragon-serpents with claws bared, their fangs threatening. Nothing here is white; everything glitters in garish, kitsch colors, bluish yellow faces, rotting tusks, bright orange hair; a gang of naked hermaphrodites couple on a smooth plane, and spurting from their genitals a herd of Cyclops with myriad arms that sweep the air, grabbing at sparks that pulse and dance, hugging weird, tangled shapes that flap about, startled, then suddenly dive into the murky space, and all the while a thin, pure gold shaft of light illuminates the vanishing points of time. Up and up I fly with the crazy-colored shapes, incapable of resisting, or grabbing onto anything. In myself I feel the simultaneous presence of all things, the world dissolving, then condensing around me, as I lose this self, as it scatters, leaking through the cells of my body, sinking into matter, unconscious, inexplicable, impossible to experience or control in this cruel void of silence and stillness.

Everything freezes. Everything goes silent. I am alone. Naked. Wild.

Dinh violently pulls me out of his painting. I tumble onto the floor, blinded by a stabbing, excruciating pain, the pain of being severed from family, loved ones, all the familiar objects that once belonged to me. I am frantic; I have fallen back into another world, the real world, the cold, white, cheerless, perfectly square world of the studio. The floor is strewn with shards of paint. My body goes limp.

I don't know when I regained consciousness, but I recognize the studio of the Bao Nghiem Tower behind the Buddhist pagoda, on the other side of Three Seas Lake, at the edge of Quy's estate. It's Thursday, New Year's Day, the Year of the Dog.

Quy climbs onto a stool to light sticks of incense in the nine bronze urns, scenting the air with a musty, sweet perfume. Staggering in and out of the heady, fragrant clouds of smoke that rise from the garden, Dinh helps me to my feet. He too seems exhausted, listless. He paints as if to torture himself, to tear himself apart. His paintings are still white, the walls are still white. Only the teapot, boiling feverishly, steam gushing from its spout, isn't white. Dinh pours tea, setting the cup on a saucer. His fingers slightly trembling, he asks me:

"What did you see?"

"I don't know. Everything."

The tea is bitter. I feel it wafting around me, the musty scent of the Turkish tea the other day. I shudder, remembering my nightmare. But the tea glides down my throat, flows into my stomach without any reaction. Dinh probably dilutes it more than Quy.

"For months now I haven't been able to paint," he says, his voice quavering with emotion. "Lots of ideas, but they refuse to take shape."

"Why?"

"Man has so many visages, so many appearances, it's impossible to express everything I feel, everything I see. It's not surprising that it's easier to do a portrait of a dead person than to represent the living. On the one hand, a corpse, a purely material object, static; on the other, a human life, with all its emotions, aspirations, dreams . . ."

As Dinh explains, he dips his paintbrush into a pot of oil. Suddenly he disappears. Like a figure in a painting that a painter simply brushes out. Erased. With one brutal, blinding white stroke of the brush, he dives and pierces the wall, right before my eyes. I call to him, run after him; I wrestle with all the wild thoughts swirling around the verandah, try to restrain them. I hear Dinh's footsteps scurrying, fleeing, then fading away. The shrill, insistent whine of the wind drags me toward the balcony overlooking rocky cliffs. Strange how this balcony opens onto another world, a world where huge stalagmites, like the blades of celestial swords, thrust into the earth. A jittery whiteness of snow careens down the mountainside toward the precipice. The stone courtyard behind the studio is deserted, buried, like a thought snuffed out, crushed under the weight of the mountains. This landscape terrifies me. Only yesterday Quy took me to the mountain, when it was still a tropical mountain teeming with mosquitoes and leeches. He told me that it hadn't changed since he crossed the Truong Son mountain range, dripping with sweat, wading through mud, rotting plants, dying for a mouthful of pure water. From the peaks of the Truong Son mountain range, the South China Sea seemed like a mirage; you could see the water, the clouds, the sky, and the earth clearly, but you couldn't touch them. American-built

Thunderchief planes lay in wait for their prey; a single step outside the jungle spelled death. Many people leapt off the cliffs into the void to die in the cool, refreshing freedom of the sea. Just yesterday Quy passionately recounted the events of the past. Just yesterday I climbed this mountain, threaded my way through the gnarled, tangled roots of the trees, under the densely woven, lush green canopy of the trees. Now an icy shroud of snow covers everything, screening off the sea, even the skyline. Not a tree, not a plant. Banks of ice as far as the eye can see. An icy, biting wind tumbles over the icy balcony railing. I run back and hide in the studio. A crazed swarm of bats, fleeing the cold, rushes in after me. Flapping wildly around the room, they crash pell-mell into walls, dash themselves against the canvases, their blood gushing, their skulls cracking. The bats panic, desperately seeking a way out. Bloody splinters of paint fly into the air. Now I understand: bats are blind, and their radar isn't working. I fling open the windows to free them. All afternoon I clean and tidy up the studio. I leave a note for Dinh:

All dreams begin with life and end in death.

During Tet, the Year of the Dog, Quy's estate is transformed. This is no vague, subtle evolution, but a visible change. The night before Tet, the Bao Nghiem Tower on the banks of Three Sea Like, the Buddhist pagoda, the altar to the ancestors, the left and right porticoes, everything rears up, monstrous. A flock of warbling sparrows slips into the chambers of the estate, the soft, shimmering dust of childhood on their wings, illuminates Quy's fifty houses with a familiar light. We have lived thousands of years with these old lintels and porticoes; we were born, we grew up, under these roofs shaped like crab shells, maturing with the columns, the colonnades, the antique panels. Moved, I gaze at the intricate woodwork. There, my face is carved into a beam. Here, my name curls around the patterns on the columns. This dawn, as limpid as a child's dream, is luminous, strangely beautiful. My body is steeped in dreams. I relive the pure, unconscious innocence of my childhood. Innocent to the point of feeling no shame when I see Quy, as if I had never stolen his wife, never ejaculated on her radiant face. That hasn't happened yet. Quy still hasn't noticed anything out of the ordinary.

Sunday, we observe the holiday with the traditional vegetarian meal. Snowflakes dance. Trees sway, wave after wave, just as they did the other day, on the balcony off Dinh's studio. Snow falls, blanketing the courtyard, tranquil, methodical, swirling around the nine urns where Quy lights incense in a cloud of smoke.

Phuong stands in front of the main pavilion in a phoenix feather coat. The dazzling, gaudy feathers glitter against her ivory skin. Chien stares at her, captivated, Phuong asks Chien to take her to the district capital to do some errands. I offer to take her, but Phuong makes a cold face. Maybe she's afraid Quy will be jealous. I don't insist. Chien's army jeep roars out the gate, leaving me behind with Quy on the vast estate.

Quy drags a stool from one urn to another, continuing to light incense. Since dawn drumbeats and loud rock music have blasted continuously from Nu's room. At noon it suddenly stops. Nu comes out into the courtyard; she's off to a demonstration against racism.

"Hey, Nu, where do you think you're going?" Quy barks.

Nu wheels around, glares at him. *"Cesse de m'appeler Nue! Mon nom est Marie!"* she snaps back. She looks like her mother: beautiful, sexy, rebellious.

Still perched on a stool, livid with anger, Quy curses her: "You little bitch, I'll kill you. Where do you think you're going like that?"

"Je vais où je veux. Je n'ai besoin de personne!"

Quy flushes with rage, his face puffy. Humiliated in front of his guest, he grabs an iron poker they use to stir the barbecue and rushes at Nu. I run after him, grab his arm back in time. "You slut!" Quy shrieks. "You heap shame on your ancestors!"

Quy is incredibly strong, and he knocks me over. But Nu has already fled past the gate. She turns around and shouts back, defiant: *"Comment puis-je m'adapter à un monde que je ne comprends pas?"*

"Ingrate!"

Quy shouts, running after her, but the bus arrives and Nu disappears. Quy's eyes still smoulder with a murky red light. Scattered snow falls and melts on the ground. Quy goes back into the house, turns on the television to watch a soccer match. The World Cup 1966, the crowds roar. I stay back, go for a stroll alone, down the porticoes. The rooms crawl with people; extended family, Quy's entourage. He has brought them here so everyone can be reunited. Every time I see them I feel like I've wandered into a zoo. Quy's cousins exhaust themselves melting down fake gold bars. His aunts and daughters-in-law and sisters-in-law work illegally sewing garments in the semidarkness, pedaling noisily on old mechanical sewing machines. They all slave away in the middle of enormous piles of merchandise. From time to time those who have finished their quota wander into the kitchen to take a break, pop their heads into the feed trough, stuff their faces, burp, and lie down in front of the television to watch a film series. In the building next door, a gaggle of nieces sing along to karaoke songs as they knit. Quy's father, the venerable Cu, sits, swinging like an old gibbon, crooning Nguyen Trai's ancient verses in Sino-Vietnamese.

"One year far from the motherland seems
like a decade . . ."

The sight of Quy's father always disorients me. He resembles an ancient beast left over from another age. A beast who slurps herbal *voi* tea and spits it on the carpet. Seeing that I don't understand, the venerable Cu frowns.

"Here in this foreign land, all that's left
me is this nostalgia that rends my
heart."

I get up abruptly and go out into the garden, sensing
that the old man is about to throw one of his temper
tantrums. Sun gleams on the peaks of the ancient,
stunted banyan tree, its languid, hairy, silvery roots.

After lunch, Quy takes me to visit the Buddhist pagoda. His anger dissipated, he forgets the scene with
Nu, becomes jovial again, proudly insisting that I take
pictures of the place. He's no artist, but he has the skill
of the photographers who still prowl around the banks
of Hoan Kiem Lake in Hanoi. He keeps talking as he
clicks the shutter. "Don't you think this looks like the
Keo pagoda, back home?"

"I thought you were from Mau Ninh."

"On my mother's side," says Quy, irritated.

He finishes the roll of Kodak film, puts away his Leica,
and motions me inside. The pagoda is small, but it has
all the essential elements: a triple outer portico, a triple
inner portico, the pavilion of the guardians of the faith,
the pavilion of celestial energy, the pavilion of great
veneration, the altar to the tutelary genie, and the bell
tower. Quy hired workers for over a year to build it.

"Looks just like the Keo pagoda in Thai Binh," I com-
pliment him.

Swelling with pride, Quy caresses the Buddha's eyes
with his trembling hands.

"I miss it terribly, you know. There was a time when my father would take me every year to the fair at the Keo pagoda; we would swim across the River Tra Ly to participate in the festivities. I won every competition: the swim meets, the duck hunts, the rice cooking. Before the end of the fair, my father would climb the tower to strike the bell and call people to prayer. . . . There were two huge bells that were cast during the Tay Son era and the statues dated back to the reign of Mac Mau Hop. I ordered them all repaired."

Quy tugs me by the shoulder, leading me toward the bell tower. He climbs the steep spiral stairs, strikes the bells three times. The ringing echoes through the forests and mountains, suddenly transporting Quy into the past. The fat on his double chin quivers, his nose twitches. Oddly, while Quy's whole body trembles, the leaves of the trees, the rocks on the mountains, begin to glow, spreading into an enormous halo of golden lacquer that covers the silver-plated sea. The echo of the bells fades, then dies out, sinking to the bottom of the still, smooth waters of the Three Seas Lake. A sad tranquility returns to the landscape. Quy's face clouds over as we leave the bell tower.

"Every year you come back to this country. And you still miss it?" I ask Quy, skeptical.

Three ideograms, the name of the pagoda, are engraved on the central column of the main pavilion: *Sacred, Light, Pagoda*. Quy slams the door, spits on the floor, sweeping the spittle aside with his shoe. "Filthy!"

Quy grumbles. "People eating and shitting everywhere. Priests and monks alike." We go into the communal house and start drinking.

"Why don't you ever go on a trip with your wife?"

"Where to?"

"To the district capital."

"What for? With those barbarians? Aren't we better off here?"

Quy empties his cup, serves more alcohol. Armagnac, Marquis de Caussade, bottled in 1971. I raise my cup, the alcohol pitches, perfumed, intoxicating. My tongue goes numb. I remember that in 1971 Chien manned an artillery base in lower Laos. Now he accompanies Quy; he can't even drink the French liquor he bartered his life for. I pity Chien. It's a lie that the survivors inherit the earth.

As the bottle empties, I start feeling drunk. Exalted, Quy proposes: "Last night the wild goats came down from the mountains. There are probably a few left here. Let's go hunting for something we can celebrate with tonight."

Quy ferrets around in his trunk, hands me an AK-47 and two sticks of dynamite. On his shoulders he carries 12.7mm machine gun and a B40 rocket launcher. The sky is clear, cloudless, the earth steeped in sunlight. Quy goes into the garage, packs the ammunition in his gleaming Mercedes 500 SEL.

"This cost me a fortune, but what a terror on the roads!" he says proudly, patting the trunk.

Looking at Quy behind the wheel, I have trouble imagining him as a soldier who once crossed the Truong Son mountain range on foot. All traces of his wounds have vanished. The road leading from Quy's estate to the mountain is narrow—here and there a power line, a mailbox, a few sign posts. The pine forest spreads as far as the eye can see. The road zigzags through rumbling waterfalls, creeks, and dales. A snake uncoils its rings, flicking through the steep rocks. Quy lights a cigarette as he crosses each pass.

"Chien trounced me brutally at cards. After you got drunk, we kept playing. I don't know how he did it, but he kept pulling hands of all dragons."

Every time we cross a pass, the car mounts, higher and higher. The peaks, still covered with snow and ice, cast dazzling reflections onto the car windows. The sharp scent of pine trees stings my nose. Cold seeths out of mountain passes choked with vegetation. Quy fumbles in his dashboard drawer, hands me a bottle of jackfruit spirits.

"I bought it back in the old country. Taste it."

The bottle is old, but as soon as I open it, it exhales the scent of a very young woman. No wonder they call this "pretty girl fruit." I swig down half the bottle, the sugar and alcohol churning in my veins. My head spins. I gaze over the cliffs and precipices, my eyes lurching in their sockets. Every time Quy takes a sharp turn, it's as if the trunk of an uprooted jackfruit tree crashes down on my body. The spines of the fruit gnaw at my gut. Quy cruises along recklessly, oblivious.

"Hey, by the way, what did you think of that Turkish tea the other day?"

"Terrifying!"

I gulp down another swig of alcohol and burp. Quy laughs, honks the horn to chase away an old blond-haired native who pushes his sheep across the road. The native mutters something, swearing at us. Quy brakes, rolls down the window, and yells at him.

"*Je t'emmerde!*"

The car continues to climb. Quy picks up our conversation.

"Anyway, that Turkish tea is extremely rare. I bought it in Ankara. In the reeducation camps in Siberia, the drug addicts used to make a really strong brew with it. A kilo of tea leaves to a cup. You drink that and it gives you the same high as drugs. Turkish tea has the same effect. *And* it's an aphrodisiac. Feeling lonely, my friend?"

Quy roars with laughter, almost chokes, lets out a long burp. A sheer wall of jagged mountain rears up in front of us. Suddenly Quy becomes taciturn, retreating into an oppressive silence. It's as if we've stumbled into another world, a place where danger stalks us, a place that Quy seems to know all too well. We get out of the car. Quy sprints ahead, slashing a path through the reeds and bamboo with his machete, almost running. From time to time he trips and turns around, signaling to me that I should follow him through the fields. Before every deserted clearing, he stares up at the sky, anxious, terrified, trying to divine some looming danger there, some disaster just waiting to fall. I'm exhausted after climbing up and down so many ravines and embankments. The worn, interminable path winds and zigzags under the spiky peaks of the white sandalwood trees. Brambles and vines grab and tear at me like thousands of black tentacles. I want to call out to Quy, ask him to stop a moment, to catch my breath, but he presses me on: "Forge ahead, quick, across the field, onward ho!"

He sprints into the clearing, his back hunched, his face tilted toward the sky, thighs and arms swimming and slashing through the reeds and ferns. He flails wildly, like an animal frantically searching for shelter. Clouds float by, lost, above the empty blue clearing. A breathtaking landscape. A wild, seething, churning river of sunlight trickles through the sky. We plunge back into the forest. Quy continues to push me on. "Hurry, the air pirates are coming!"

There, they appear. Just as Quy stops speaking. In the middle of the clearing. An indescribable beauty. We are both awed, dumbfounded. This is no ordinary beauty; it has the sparkle of legend, the deep mystery of tradition: an ancient beauty, like a family portrait, an heirloom handed down from generation to generation. A popular painting carefully preserved through the centuries. From the ancient, glittering river of light rises the iridescent silhouette of a mythical being: a hundred dragons harmoniously undulating, like a hundred young girls dancing with silk scarves. They are part legend, part reality. They coil and then rear, dance, frolic, play, toss each other balls of flame that fly up, flapping, light as eggshells, flower petals floating on air and fire. A bewitching beauty. It comes back to me in a rush, a deep serenity that I had lost a long time ago: *They are still alive. They haven't forgotten me, they've followed me here.*

Suddenly, from out of nowhere, rain. Drenching rain of the flood season. Yes, I recognize it, this warm, soothing rain, from another time, another life. I see myself running, carefree, joyful, through the back alleys. Rain welcomes me, greets me at every horizon. Jubilant, joyful rain. Up to my knees. Earth and sky dissolve into one wavy, frantically shivering lake. The yellowed walls, once whitewashed with lime, are suddenly covered with slick, glistening wet moss; they laugh and beckon to me, guiding my steps to the threshold of the temple. The temple to the Hung kings. Majestic, monumental, awe-inspiring, like in the epic poems. They are there too, perched on the rooftops, imposing yet familiar. I have known them since childhood, when Mother still carried me to the pagoda in her arms to draw a bamboo stick that told your fortune. Dragons greet me warmly, beating the tails in the air. On each pillar, in the corner of each pagoda, a sweet little dragon waits for me, wriggling his whiskers, eagerly twitching his snout, smiling. I speak to them, give them names, like close friends: Hoanh, Thanh, Hoa. I wave. They wag their tails. At night they would always come down from the sky, toward me, accompanying me in my dreams. Sometimes, without thinking, I would flip through a history book. They would print themselves on the pages, coil at my feet. All through my childhood we never left each other.

Rain drenches my face, refreshes my memory. But I see that they are weeping. They've come back in flesh and blood to reveal themselves to me. The dragons are moved to find me here, a thousand leagues from our homeland. I want to call out to Quy, to tell him about the love that has linked us across the oceans for all these long years.

But Quy lifts up his machine gun. I watch, horrified, as he feeds bullets down the steel barrel. I scream, appalled. I throw myself at Quy, clutch and pull at him. I wrestle with him, shrieking, throwing myself at his feet, begging, praying. But with a swift kick, Quy knocks me flat, spraying the dragons with machine gunfire. Bullets snap, lashing and stinging, ripping through the clearing, boring into the dragons' flesh. Scars of fire. I hear shrill, awful howling. Blood gushes, stains the sky, spreading in a crimson pool across the horizon. Their twisted, entangled corpses fall onto the grass. Quy keeps spraying the clearing with bullets amidst the moans and cries. In agony, I scream and sob, throw myself on Quy again, clawing at him, but he shoves me off. Again, I hurl myself at him. The little dragons collapse.

Then I see a child, a young man, bleeding from the nose and ears, trying to flee the clearing. He crawls, holding his guts in his hands, staining the earth purple with a stream of his blood. Quy pushes me over, sets off the dynamite, and to finish the carnage, he shoots off a B40. Mortar shards fly toward the dying boy, shearing off his outstretched, supplicating hands. He dies, right there, under the white clouds, on the green grass. His blood, limbs, head, guts, scattered.

There are crimes that kill the human in us as soon as we commit them. But worse yet is another crime: to not know that we commit crimes. Quy belongs to the second category of criminals. And me? I—I who witness— to which category of criminals do I belong?

I was still searching for my name on the list of crimes when Dinh died on New Year's Day. His naked body lies stretched on a huge white jute canvas, as large as the floor. The studio is smeared with paint. Dinh must have bathed himself in it, must have thrashed about on that canvas before dying. His face is battered, wizened, but through the crack of his eyelids flickers the serenity of a man who made the irrevocable decision to go. Since the day of the dragon hunt, a haunting sadness weighs on the fifty residences of Quy's estate. A melancholy from who knows where, who knows why—it wasn't Dinh's death—seems to shroud every house.

We bury Dinh in indifference and boredom. Quy gnaws and sucks at a few moldy dragon bones still lying around. Chien shuffles the cards. Phuong, seated under a flame tree, absently embroiders complicated designs on a silk slip. Alone, I dig the earth, lift heaping shovels of gold real gold, in eighteen carats, the kind that exists only on this continent—and toss them over Dinh, covering his stomach with it. His body is bound hastily in white jute cloth, the same white jute canvas he had painted all his life yet never finished. I raise a stone stele, scribble a few words in memoriam: *Enjoyed life . . . left the world . . . eternal regrets.*

I wash my hands in Three Seas Lake and return to the table. Here, where we played our ruthless card games, where we had our raucous drinking parties, where our grandiose ambitions were born. Now all that's left is a vague, monotonous sadness, an unhappiness that is formless yet so real that it rises in the steam from our bowls of watery cabbage soup. We don't talk anymore. We just look at each other, indifferent, like stones, blocks of wood. Quy has lost his zeal, his enthusiasm. Chien looks like what he is: an old soldier who lost a twenty-year war in one day's battle, then did ten years in prison, only to be airbrushed out of the history of this century. Phuong, the most seductive of all women, has lost her sex appeal. Her voluptuous body still arouses desire, but when I slip my hand inside her blouse to fondle her breasts, she coldly pushes it away.

"Try that again and I'll call old Quy," Phuong hisses between her teeth. She is aggressive, ice cold. Ashamed, I blush, pull back my hand, lower my head, slipping a fearful glance in old Quy's direction. Quy doesn't react, and though he hears everything, he just glances up at the empty, sullen sky, as if waiting for something to happen, or for some beast to appear. He is suffering, as if he had just lost his family tree.

Chien takes the officer's cordons off his uniform, wipes the gilded lead threads, corroded by rust. His uniform, the one he used to wear for the memorial ceremonies at the War Square, is now so tight he can't even close the buttons over his belly. Phuong gazes indifferently at the fat that bulges at Chien's belly. Her desire is gone. We are all dazed, haunted by the memory of our New Year's banquet of dragon meat. That night Chien and Phuong brought back tons of watermelons from the district capital, huge firecrackers and brandied fruit. Quy had cut up the dragon with an electric saw. The fresh, bloody red meat of that baby dragon, glistened, still bursting with youth. It was horrible to look at. But I couldn't resist the temptation, the thrill of tasting fresh, unfrozen dragon flesh for the first time. I helped Quy boil the meat, then roll it in paper-thin rice pancakes while Phuong minced lemon grass and chilies and crushed pineapple to add to the fish sauce. Chien cut the thighs into pieces for kebabs. Phuong grilled the rice pancakes to accompany a few local specialties: a dragon fondue, a dragon tripe stew, grapefruit dragon tripe salad, dragon in aspic, and three plates of steamed baby dragon kidneys. Quy cut off the head to make stock for a green bean rice porridge that he saved to eat later, with dinner. We feasted and drank, made the ritual visits to the neighbors and extended family, crossing thresholds littered with red firecracker wrappings.

It's only on New Year's Day that everyone discovers a mute, long-repressed sadness. A melancholy that withers the heart and guts. A grief that wizens the flesh, gnaws at the bones. A poison that seeps into the soul. The world is empty, meaningless. Life is a chain of despair chasing after a happiness that never arrives. Nighttime is a long, hard, barren dream. Days begin with a bleak, sunless dawn that holds no future. We live like the condemned. In our hearts we know that we have committed the crime of parricide and that we are waiting for our punishment. It arrives that night, when Nu comes back from the demonstration against racism. She walks up to the dinner table, stands there, defiant.

"Je veux m'en aller d'ici."

"Where do think you're going?" snaps Quy, furious.

"Je pars avec mon mec," Nu continues, her face hard, rebellious.

"What boyfriend?" Quy grumbles. Phuong jumps to her feet. Nu retreats, avoiding Quy's hand, which stretches out to grab her hair.

"Il est Turc. C'est un immigré comme vous. Il vit en Allemagne; je veux partager sa vie."

"You're staying at *this* house. I forbid you to sleep with Turks."

Quy grabs Nu by the hair, pins down her head, slaps her hard, over and over. Nu struggles and sobs, but the more she struggles, the harder Quy beats her.

"Take that, you tramp!"

"Vous êtes dégeulasses. Vous aussi, vous êtes des immi-grés! Des Turcs!"

Nu struggles, but Phuong runs to Quy's aid, brandishing an electric cord, and whips Nu's face, forbidding her to respond. Quy ties up his daughter, drags her into the first-floor room, and double-locks it. Nu's jade bracelet lies broken on the floor. I pick it up, and I feel a strange desire bursting in my palm. Quy comes back down, grim, wallowing in his arid sadness, in the memory of his remote ancestors, nostalgia for a happiness aborted since the extinction of the familiar dragon race. To kill time Chien absently shuffles the cards. Phuong listlessly darns a slip. Quy's aunts keep up their feverish black-market garment production. The voice of venerable old Cu echoes in the distance, reciting an ancient poem:

> Already my hair is gray, my eyes fail me.

I go off in search of the source of this new passion that has just blossomed in me. No discovery is more exciting than the discovery of childhood.

Nu waits for me in her room. Her shiny, young girl's

hair cascades down the back of her white linen blouse. My passion is dizzying, beautiful, as intoxicating as the adolescence on the dreamy oval of Nu's face. An innocent look. A fold of silk discreetly hides her breasts. Nu is pretty, like girls at the age when they still put a barette in their hair to go to class, and that I used to wait for in front of the high school not so long ago. Fine, smiling lips, romantic, misty eyes, a tiny, timid nose. An entire sky filled with flowers, lost dreams illuminates my soul. Moved, I grab Nu's hand, squeeze it in mine.

"You haunt me."

"Why did you come so late?" Nu says, startled, glancing at me shyly. I shiver with happiness. Nu speaks my mother tongue. I had always hoped she wouldn't speak to me in the indigenous language. Her shoulders tremble when I pull her into my arms. I embrace her passionately, deeply, nervously. I kiss her full lips, but Nu pushes me away, murmuring: "Tell my parents to let me go live with Mohammed in Germany."

My heart sinks. So, Nu still loves that damned Turkish guy. Shouting and quarreling sounds rise from the garden. Chien is berating Quy for having killed the most beautiful of beasts. Quy insults Chien for having invited the beasts to trample the tombs of our ancestors. Suddenly, a burst of gunfire. The crackling of American M16s mixed with a hail of Russian AKs. The 155mm cannons roar, while the 130mm cannons thunder from the mountains, their mortars crashing down on Quy's estate. Walls crack and crumble. Ceilings and floors buckle and cave in with each explosion. It's June 19, the anniversary of the founding of the Armed Forces of the Republic of Vietnam; it's also September 2, anniversary of the historic proclamation of independence at Ba Dinh Square. I jump, horrified. The war has come back. New Year's Day isn't over yet, the truce is still on, but already flames lick at the verandah. Nu cries out for help. I run into the garden. Chien is dousing gasoline on the Supreme Ancestor Temple, launching phosphorous grenades. He sets fire to the temple. I try to stop him. "Have you gone crazy?"

"Shut up! This temple belongs to Quy's family! I'm burning it! *The fatherland springs from the barrels of our rifles!*" He sounds his trumpet, setting the rhythm to march: *Our bayonets gleam with hatred, the hatred of slavery*. The garden is deserted. Phuong has disappeared, who knows where. I run toward the Buddhist pagoda in search of Quy. But I spot him fishing a trunk out of Three Seas Lake filled with bazookas, mortars, mines, and TNT.

"The war is over! Why are you shooting each other?" I shout over to him.

"Shut up, kid. You don't understand anything! I'm going to kill him!" Quy arms himself with a bazooka, and aims mortars at the very spot where Chien and I are standing. Explosions shower down on the houses in front of the Bao Nghiem Tower, which bursts into flames. I realize that Nu is still locked in her room on the first floor, which has just burst into flames. Delirious, as if possessed, Quy bombards us, the whites of his eyes rolled back. "Advance on Saigon! Wipe out the enemy!" I race up the stairs, suddenly aroused. Nu's hair changes color, I see it clearly. Golden blond curls unfurl and bob on her cling T-shirt. Nu is no different from any other native teenage girl. Her pert, inviting breasts excite me.

I grab her, clutch her in my arms. Military music thunders through the room as Chien sets off the fireworks for the troop exercises. *The Northern bandits have come to atrociously massacre the people. Binh Long, my native land, is littered with their graves next to the rows of Soviet T54 tank carcasses.* I rip off Nu's shirt, exposing her child's skin, bite her soft white breasts, her tender pink nipples. It's New Year's Eve, the eve of 1968, the Year of the Monkey—they are burying us alive in common graves. It's late afternoon in My Lai village, the hour of unspeakable massacre. Tomorrow is the day the pirates who stalk the boat people exult in mass rape. Phuong's voice rises, a shrill, icy soprano from the back of the garden: *Evenings I stroll along the hills, I sing above the corpses,* she sings, then screams, "Give me back my child!" Then Quy's voice, in chorus, from behind the Buddhist pagoda, *Kill the torturers, annihilate the heinous American invaders! Rise* up, patriots! To arms, into the streets beside our beloved soldiers." Mortars from the 122mm rain down on Cai Lay College. I see tails of flame slice through the air in front of Nu's window. I rip off her panties. I want to possess her happy, fulfilled, confident youth, this youth free of fear of the future. I want to tear up the diploma she will get, smash her spontaneity, the innocence of this body that knows nothing of bullets and bombs. I want her childhood to be as painful as mine. Flames soar up in a blinding flash. Nu tries to cover her breasts, her stomach, with her hands; she begs and pleads with me. But I grab her by the hair, push her head back down on the bed, twist her arms behind her back, open my fly. Her body is a tender white, spread before me like a rice paddy bent under the weight of ripe, plump grains. *Stand up! Heroic people of South Vietnam!* Quy's voice shatters my eardrums. Chien barks into the loudspeakers, rolling the drums, sounding the trumpets: *The Van Lang empire flows in our veins, irrigating our flesh and bones with the blood of our ancestors.* I pierce Nu with all my strength, body and soul. Her blood flows scarlet, the blood of the babies, the children who died in My Lai village, at Cai Lai elementary school. I thrust my sharp, enormous spear deep, deep into her, ripping her flesh, severing her nerves, tearing her muscles. Nu twists and screams in pain. She sobs as I twist her arms behind her back, up to her shoulders. Flames devour the room, inflames the mosquito net, the covers, the mat. Bullets crackle all around us. Phuong cries out, her voice hoarse, cracking, "Give me back my child!" Quy intones the "Hymn to Solidarity." Chien raises his operatic, impassioned tenor voice: *Our flag floats, majestic, over our beloved city, reconquered during the night with our blood.*

I plunge farther into Nu, all the way to the tenderest part of her. Like you would butcher an animal. A water buffalo, a cow, a dog. *Evenings I stroll along the hills, I sing above the corpses.* I want to live this war. Participate. Take part in the crime. Face up to it. Take responsibility. I want to see *"the graves that engulf the bodies of my brothers"* with my own eyes. For once I want to kill someone, know the intoxication of shooting a man that Chien and Quy always talk about, that they say they will never forget. I rape her, savagely. I pillage her childhood, kill it, degrade her mother, her father. I desecrate her youth. And I am satisfied.

Years later, after that Tet, the Year of the Dog, I return to Quy's estate. The four celestial pillars still standing barely come up to eye level. The estate has been razed, burned to the ground, abandoned. Ashes stirred by the wind carry a slight stench, the lingering scent of the Holy War. Quy's estate has changed. The primitive forests that once engulfed it have disappeared, yielding their place to mini-hotels and inns that clutter the mountainside. Even the beach has vanished. All that's left are rows of food stalls with English signs advertising SEA FOOD. Four or five streets are packed with car-rental shops, travel agencies, places to rent summer villas. I cross the grandiose triple gate, the last vestige of the days of Tet, the Year of the Dog. Everything is deserted. The fifty houses razed by the fire still haven't been rebuilt. I remember now: Chien and Quy were sentenced to twenty years in prison for having set fire to the forest; they are still serving their time. I was condemned to ten years for rape of a minor. Phuong married a native and Nu a foreigner. Ashes swirl in the wind, then fall gently back to earth. Someone dug up Dinh's tomb to steal the paintings on the jute canvases. They broke my stele. All that's left is a hole only about a hand deep. I take off my raincoat. I light sticks of incense, plant them in the mound of dirt covering the tomb. It's as if I'd never left, never left these dilapidated, ravaged dwellings. I no longer dream about emigrating. I trample weeds and grasses as tall as I am, that no one has bothered to cut, under my feet. There's a billboard on the only piece of cleared land. I read the starting price for a public offering; they're building an estate reserved for South Koreans. I lift the lid to the mailbox, see a scrap of paper with a few words scrawled in Nu's handwriting: *Heard you were coming back to X. I came by, but you weren't there. What happened happened a long time ago. I'm not angry anymore. I'm living happily with Mohammed.*

The wind whistles past the nine bronze urns, still

standing, stoic, solitary, the mournful sigh of a bygone era. On one of the columns, the venerable old Cu has engraved a verse from a famous poem by Nguyen Trai:

> In youth, the sweet scent of our success
> perfumes the entire literary forest . . .

For the first time I understand the meaning of this verse, written six centuries ago. And I can almost smell it somewhere, ever so faintly, the elusive scent of the forest.

NOTES FROM
THE AUTHOR

Since 1979, I have lived as a refugee in France. I have met Vietnamese war veterans of the defeated Republic of Vietnam army in their communities in California and in France, and found them enclosed in their own surreal, lost world. They are obsessed with their defeat, never having gotten over it, and yet they are also in denial about it. They continue to wage the war, at least in their minds. When I first returned to Vietnam in 1994, I discovered their mirror image on the other side: an identical community of war veterans, who in the meantime have become ultraconservative, still re-enacting their heroic battles. More than twenty years later, my generation still lives with their interminable wars. Whether we came of age in Hanoi, Saigon, New York, Los Angeles, Melbourne, or Paris, we're too young to have participated in the bloody games, but we're old enough to have suffered from them, to be conscious of Vietnam's tragedies. In my stories, people undergo terrible transformations, from being victims, abandoned, to being rapists, torturers of others. This is what can happen to us in war, I have noticed.

THE CORAL REEF

(This adaptation of an autobiographical novella first appeared in *Granta: Fifty*, Summer 1995.)

I wrote this story the way I lived it, without knowing what would happen to me, without being master of my fate. The crossing, aside from the nightmare of becoming a "boat person," was my first real contact with Vietnamese society. Up until the day I left, I had never gone far from my family, the road that led from my mother's house to school. I only knew other school children my age, from the same social class: southern-ers (or northern immigrants to the South after the French departure), merchants, partisans of the Repub-lic of Vietnam. All of a sudden on the boat, I dis-covered the complexities of this hybrid society of

Vietnamese and Chinese, the friction between our cultures, our ways of behaving. I also found out how cruel people can be to each other, an experience that has left me changed.

GUNBOAT ON THE YANGTZE

I saw this film on television in France (original English title, *The Sand Pebbles*). An adolescent at the time, a refugee just off the boat, I was struck by the last words of the sailor, played by Steve McQueen, before he dies in the courtyard of a remote Chinese temple. Perhaps like him, I thought, I will die a thousand leagues from home, from my country, without ever understanding why.

THE BACK STREETS OF HOI AN

I have never been to Hoi An, once a bustling, cosmopolitan port city in central Vietnam, but this is the way I imagine it now: moribund, forgotten, effaced. A place whose musty silence makes you feel the drip of time, like an excruciating, slow death. Hoi An also hides a guilty secret: for fourteen centuries it was the sacred heartland of the Cham people before their civilization was wiped out by the Vietnamese in their expansion toward the South. Behind its ancient walls, Hoi An barely contains the rage of centuries, the powerlessness.

Nha Nam

Nha Nam, which means "Delicate South," is both ancient Vietnam with all its barbaric traditions, and Vietnam today, as it appears to me, disfigured by the ravages of a primitive market economy. I began this story in Saigon in 1995, after surviving a motorcycle crash. I had just read the story "Nha Nam Rain" by Nguyen Huy Thiep, a famous contemporary Vietnamese writer. Other than the title, our two stories have nothing in common, though I quote a few lines from the beginning of Thiep's story at the end of mine—and made Thiep the central character. I also had fun mimicking his style. The verses in the story are excerpts from the poetry of the famous fifteenth-century poet and military hero Nguyen Trai, decapitated along with three generations of his family by the dynasty that sainted him. Before his death, he retreated from public life and became a hermit, writing poetry in a forest called Con Son outside of Hanoi. For me, Nguyen Trai symbolizes the fate of Vietnamese writers and artists.

The Dragon Hunt

[Originally titled "Turkish Dream"]

According to a legend that every Vietnamese child knows by heart, our first king descended from a dragon and a fairy. We are "the sons of the dragon."

The Dragon Lord Lac Long was our first hero; he saved us from demons and foreign invaders from the North. But we are also the children, the survivors, of a divorce: half of us followed our father to the delta in the South, while half of us remained with our mother in the mountains of the North.

"The Dragon Hunt" is about this rupture, this growing and yet ancient divide between North and South, between Vietnamese in Vietnam and those of us who left, between the generations. The Vietnamese people no longer share the same past, and because we don't, our future is uncertain. By putting the beast to death, we also put to death a myth about ourselves. And when the myth is gone, the childhood legend over, we lose our bearings. Killing dragons is at once an act of fratricide and self-destruction.

About the

Author

Born in Saigon in 1962, Tran Vu left Vietnam by boat at the age of sixteen with his elder brother. When his boat of 400 people was shipwrecked on a coral reef, he escaped by diving through a porthole and for ten days survived in the water with a life jacket given to him by his mother, who stayed behind in Vietnam. After he was rescued, Tran Vu spent a year in the Palawan refugee camp in the Philippines before the Red Cross brought him to France in December 1979. Still a minor and without a word of French when he arrived, Tran

Vu was housed in a series of state orphanages and was put through high school and college by the French government. He now lives in Paris, where he works as a computer analyst.

Tran Vu has published two collections of short stories in Vietnamese with overseas Vietnamese publishers in the United States. His work has appeared in English in *Granta* and in two anthologies of Vietnamese fiction in translation.